ANTIPHONY

CHRIS KATSAROPOULOS

LUMINIS BOOKS

LUMINIS BOOKS
Published by Luminis Books
1950 East Greyhound Pass, #18, PMB 280,
Carmel, Indiana, 46033, U.S.A.
Copyright © Chris Katsaropoulos, 2012

PUBLISHER'S NOTICE

This is a work of fiction. Names, characters, places, and incidents are either the product of the author's imagination or are used fictitiously. Any resemblance to actual persons, living or dead, business establishments, events, or locales is entirely coincidental.

Cover art for *Antiphony* courtesy NASA.

ISBN-10: 1-935462-33-4
ISBN-13: 978-1-935462-33-0

Printed in the United States of America

10 9 8 7 6 5 4 3 2 1

The courage of the poet is to keep ajar the door that leads into madness.

—*Christopher Morley*

1

THEODORE SEES NOW that he should have brought sunglasses, for even here, within the gaping, hushed volume of the convention hotel lobby, splinters of irretrievable light reach through the wall of glass that defines the reception area and make him squint, as he tries to focus on what his wife is telling him.

"The cooking class is at one," she is saying, "then I'm going to the spa for a massage." His wife Ilene, young enough still to make other men look twice. Yet enough of a wife to make him sometimes want to look away. "So I probably won't see you until dinner."

He had not realized until this moment that he has been jealous of her the entire journey. "You'll miss my presentation. That was part of the reason for coming here." When she had suggested two months ago joining him for his trip to present a paper at the New International Perspectives on String Theory Symposium in Santa Rosa, it had seemed like a good opportunity for the two of them to spend a weekend away, an expense account vacation to break up the tedium of a Midwestern winter. But he has not been able to relax and enjoy the trip the same way she has. When she ordered her second glass of wine on the plane and then her third glass of wine at dinner last night, the prospect of standing at the podium in front of a room filled with anyone who matters in the incestuous and backbiting world of particle physics made him balk and ask for a diet soda instead. And now she is telling him that she has planned to have a stranger kneading her naked back at the moment of his supreme triumph, when he delivers the conclusion of the speech that will cement his reputation as one of the leading thinkers in Perturbation Theory, an important but, in his view, still entirely underappreciated offshoot of String Theory.

"The main reason," she says, always able to discern the thinly-veiled insecurities that motivate his actions. "You wanted me to see you on stage. Performing." She touches him lightly on the forearm. "Not that I don't want to, I'm very proud. But I wouldn't understand a word you're saying. And this was the only time I could sign up for the class."

A ray of sunlight catches on the golden fan of hair that drapes her shoulder. As he contemplates these shimmering filaments of hair, they seem strangely detached from Ilene, they have become merely one more sleek, clean object in the lobby of the hotel, whose only purpose seems to manifest the wonder of the solemn late-winter light pouring in from the two-story windows. What a volume of light! Theodore often catches himself undertaking mental calculations regarding the physics of light as he watches it achieve one of its many visual tricks, transforming an item such as Ilene's hair or the cut glass vase on the registration desk into a display of pure sculptured form.

He knows, as a matter of fact, that there are 400 photons per cubic centimeter scattered throughout the entire universe, a suffusion of light permeating every ounce of space that exists as a remnant of the background radiation from the Big Bang. Even in the darkest midnight, we are literally bathed in light. And that thought, coupled with the tremendous intensity of the glare from the early-afternoon sun, leads him to one of his favorite thought-pictures, envisioning himself inhabiting a universe that is abundantly full rather than empty. It is natural for us to feel that we are moving through the open air, a vast empty sky or even a clear open space such as this lobby, but really we are more or less bathed in an ocean of energy, even the blank vacuum of intergalactic space filled with quantum particles that randomly pop in and out of being. There is so much energy all around us that he has to laugh when news show pundits blather on about the doom and gloom of the latest energy crisis and the price of gasoline hitting four dollars a gallon.

Everything is energy; it is only a matter of harnessing it. Every cubic centimeter of space has enough energy locked inside to power the city of Santa Rosa for a hundred years.

And this brings him back again to his favorite thought problem of recent days. He has been fiddling with the idea of how many photons can fit in a cubic centimeter of space—not how many are always there as a remnant of the background radiation, but how many can be crammed into a discrete volume of space? As the problem first caught his attention, he thought it would be a quick one to solve, but it is trickier than he might have imagined. He has been juggling it in his mind for the past week, and has thought about lobbing it at Pradeep Malawar, one of his friends at the Institute for Cosmological Physics, but he guesses that Pradeep will have a pat answer for it, cut and dried in the smug way so many of his colleagues have that they are right about all the basic premises of physics. So Theodore has kept it to himself, working it around in his head like a child's long-lost toy, playing with it from different angles.

Is there a limit to the number of photons that can pour through these big plate glass windows at any given moment?

Instinctively, his mind tells him yes, because there is a limit to what can be measured, and also because if you squeeze too much energy into a particular volume of space, you will form a black hole. However, individual photons can have a wide range of energies, so when you go to the lowest energy level, you can greatly increase the number of photons you cram in. Another problem: When you smash a lot of photons together, they form a collective entity that cannot easily be redivided into unique parts again. In some ways, the problem is a bit like trying to determine how many drops can come from a glass of water, or how many angels can fit on the head of a pin.

Theodore knows that thinking about this is silly in a way— this should all be very basic, the kind of thing Pradeep would never bother to consider because he takes so many of the fundamentals for granted. But when Theodore lets his mind wander like this, probing the margins of elementary premises, he sometimes stumbles upon a new way of looking at things that brings him a hint of insight on a totally different problem, perhaps even one that is pertinent to his research. As his mind wanders, he watches a young boy, maybe seven years old, hurl a football along a perfectly calculated parabolic arc across the lobby towards another boy, who from the looks of him must be his brother, the ball zipping upward to the point at the top of the curve where gravity overtakes the forward acceleration of the ball and begins to drag it down. Even at this age, the boy innately knows the perfect amount of force to apply from his arm and hand flinging forward and also the perfect angle and direction to launch the ball, in an instant taking into account the drag applied by the molecules of air, and also the lift from the spiraling rotation of the ball, which helps keep it afloat longer.

In the next instant, the ball lands in the outstretched hands of the other boy, the brother, his fingertips clutching it, holding on. And that image, of the ball landing safely, along with the intrusive thought of his research, nudges Theodore into a vague realization that he is missing something.

Yes, he *is* missing something. His notes, for the presentation, two college-ruled sheets of paper filled with scribblings that only he could read or understand. He has been dreading the presentation now for weeks, and those pieces of paper have been his crutch, a distillation of everything he wants to tell the ballroom full of his colleagues about the work he has been doing for the past six years, including all the key formulas that culminate in the breakthrough that is the reason for his paper getting published—and the professional accolades that will come with it. The computer slides he has created to embellish the talk are some help, but they don't have all the detail he needs.

Without those notes, he's sunk.

He pats himself on the front of his thighs, to check whether the notes are in the pockets of his slacks, but he feels nothing but the tautness of his quadriceps on one side and his plump leather wallet on the other. He reaches inside his sportscoat and checks the vest pocket, but it holds only his cell phone and the key card to their hotel room. He tries to place his hand in the outside pockets of the jacket, but these are still sewn shut, so rarely does he dress formally, even to this extent, without a suit or a tie, his shirt collar open to the first button.

"What is it?" Ilene has become accustomed, over the years, to his episodes of panic when he discovers he has lost something. It barely warrants a mention from her.

"My notes," he says, glaring at her as if she might have taken them. "I must have left them in the room." He looks around the lobby of the hotel for a clock, but can find none. Why is it that there are never any clocks in large public places? A momentary curse lifted against the unthoughtful designers of the hotel rises to his lips, then passes away unsaid. "What time is it?"

Ilene checks her watch and seeks to reassure him. "No hurry. You have eighteen minutes." But she also cannot resist this opportunity to get a jab in. "Maybe you should wear a watch." She studies hers again as if she has just discovered the wonder of its efficient functioning. "You're always late. Don't you care about time?"

"I do," Theodore says, "in a conceptual way. I'm fascinated by it."

This is not a problem, he thinks, seeking to adopt Ilene's confident attitude about the situation—there is always plenty of time. He glances at one of the flowers propped against the rim of the glass vase and thinks he can see the petals move, just slightly, unfurling their tender lavender tips as if grasping at the light of the sun. But perhaps he is only imagining this—they are not real. It must be only a current of air disturbed by the two football-playing boys as they run past that has caused the flowers to move.

"If you don't have them, they must be in the room." Ilene releases a heavy sigh that seems to enfold all the exasperation of living with someone as willfully impractical as her husband over the years. "Want me to run up and get them?"

"No, I'll go." He does not want to ruin her trip, even if it means ruining his. She has had her heart set on this class, the massage, an afternoon of indulgence. "I have plenty of time. I think I know where I left them." Yet even as he says this, a slippery feeling of dread starts to build within the pit of his stomach. He has no idea where the notes are, and without them he must rely on his own very shaky memory to supply the details necessary to fill an hour and twenty-five minutes of empty time in front of an audience of his peers. He has never liked talking to more than a couple of people at once, so he clings to the memory of what an undergrad professor of his once said upon completing a very brief fifteen minute lecture and letting the class out early to enjoy the remainder of the spring day: "Tell them what you're going to say, say it, then tell them what you said." It seems like a sound method of public speaking, one he has intended to follow during his preparation for the meeting, but without his notes it may be impossible for him to do.

He casts his eyes at Ilene, hoping she might somehow supply a resolution to his predicament, as she has done so many times before. Her green eyes look past him, over his shoulder, towards the street outside the hotel. She is taller than he is by several inches, and that has always been in his mind an indicator of the underlying basis of their relationship: He is always looking up at the sky towards her, and she is always looking down at the earth towards him. While he has been lost in contemplation of the intricate workings of interstellar space, she has raised the children, cooked the meals, and paid the bills. Today, her hair is flipped out at the ends in a style he has never seen before. In anticipation of this trip, she must have splurged on a new haircut as well as the outfit she is wearing, a gauzy blouse overlaid with rhomboidal patterns of green and yellow that remind him of the arabesque on the back of a playing card. If he delays her, she will be all dressed up with no place to go. Once she made the decision to join him on the trip, she must have been looking forward to it very much, planning what she would wear each day and selecting, after much deliberation, this particular outfit in anticipation of this afternoon. He does not want the trip to be a disappointment to her—one more in a series of disappointments.

After they married, Ilene wondered if it might be better for him to take a job at a large corporation, an aerospace firm perhaps, doing practical, applied science and getting paid handsomely for it. But he had been determined to carry on with his dream of uncovering the inner workings of the universe, peeling back, layer by layer, the laws of time and space and gravity that hold everything together and make it all work the way it does. He had a feeling, as had so many other young physicists of his day, that they were ninety-eight percent of the way to a final solution, a grand unifying theory that could boil everything down to a handful of equations, or even one very simple, eloquent equation, that sums it all up in a kind of primal algebraic ju-jitsu, like one of those children's toys that start out as a colorful geodesic sphere of interlocking plastic rods and can collapse upon itself into a single, unitary ball. So, he insisted on chasing the dream as a pure scientist and ended up at the Institute for Cosmological Physics on a research fellowship, earning less than many high school teachers, locking Ilene in to a life of making ends meet, cutting coupons and shopping for specials at the wholesale club, and trying to enjoy a trip to a physics conference now and then as if it were a real family vacation. Even though they are now well past the financial struggles of raising their two children, who have been comfortably launched into well-paying careers of their own, this intimation of the life he has inflicted on her magnifies the feeling he has of an impending doom. He reaches his hand out and touches the filmy fabric of her sleeve.

"Have fun at the class. This won't take long."

She brings her eyes back to him and grants him a smile. Though she has thickened at the waist in her middle age and her small-boned angel's face has acquired the puffiness of an extra chin when she looks down at him, the individual features he fell in love with, the pursed rosebud lips, the nose tipped up like a miniature ski jump, the startling green eyes, are still there. "You'll knock their socks off."

As he steps away from her, he glimpses the boys on the opposite side of the lobby, tossing the football once more in a semblance of a play they must be reenacting, and he remembers another number that brings him back to the problem of the photons. To know how many photons can fit into a cubic centimeter, you would have to put a time parameter around the answer, because photons are not static objects—a photon never stands still and it can only go at the speed of light. Like all other particles in the universe, photons have both wave-like and particle-like properties. He imagines his mythical cubic centimeter of space as a small transparent box being inundated from every direction by a series of waves of light, from a myriad of sources, like ripples in a pond, and so he would have to limit the duration of the thought-problem to some arbitrary amount of time, such as one second. And then he would be able to say that the wavelength of one photon is equal to the Planck length, which is the smallest possible length in the universe: 1.6×10^{-35} meters. The Planck length is the distance a photon travels in a Planck time, which is the shortest possible time in the universe. So, from here he can simply divide a cubic centimeter by the Planck length and divide a second by the Planck time, multiply those two numbers together, and voilà, he has his answer. The calculations would only take a couple of minutes to set up on a laptop computer.

Having reduced this problem to a set of easily knowable computations, he sets forth down the corridor that leads to the elevator that will lift him to his hotel room and his notes. He is reassured by the fact that everything is knowable—everything can be found.

This hallway is much dimmer than the main lobby, and it takes his eyes a moment to adjust. There is a quiet, muffled air here, away from the hubbub of people checking in or checking out and bellmen hoisting luggage onto their gleaming brass carts.

Then, as his pupils widen to allow a few more particles of light in, the problem of his little transparent cubic centimeter box comes at him again from another, more philosophical angle. The thought that enters his head is disturbing enough that he mentally holds it away from himself for a moment, a horrifying sight he must avoid seeing. Is it not true, according to quantum theory, that the probability wave of each photon fills the entire universe? So, when he looks at it from that perspective, the answer to the problem jumps from a certain discrete, knowable number all the way to infinity.

How many photons can fit in a cubic centimeter?

The answer is... all of them.

This is the kind of maddening thought that keeps him awake at night. The job of the physicist must have been so easy in the days before relativity and quantum theory were conjured up to wrestle with each other at opposite ends of the physical scale of the universe. Every time he feels he has an answer to a problem like this he is toying with, it seems to flip around on itself and turn into something entirely different, depending on which way he is looking at it, like the snake that circles around to eat its own tail. The thought of all the photons in the universe crowding into his little see-through box has released a slippery sensation in his abdomen; a set of heavy, wet washrags, it seems, are sliding against one another in his gut, and he is suddenly seized by a tremendous urge to defecate, just as the bell sounds its beckoning tone and the doors to the elevator slither open. Perhaps he can get in and make it up to his room. He calculates a moment and decides against it. He really does have to go—now.

Fearing the worst, Theodore looks around for a bathroom, there must be one nearby. There, just down the hall. He strides quickly towards the paired doors and charges into the bright, tiled room, grateful to find that all the stalls are empty. He slides the bolt into place and drops his trousers to the floor, twisting his boxers around the dark socks on his ankles as he falls back upon the toilet seat with not a moment to spare, the contents of his bowels spilling into the echoing bowl full of water with a thundering sound loud enough that he wonders whether anyone outside the bathroom can hear it.

Lately, he has found himself to be ravenous, eating a huge meal for dinner, like the steak he had last night, and following it up with another big meal for breakfast—two eggs over easy, sausage links, bacon, toast, juice and coffee—and he wonders where it all goes. He hasn't gained an ounce. He has always had a tight-knit, wiry sort of body, but he's been eating twice as much as usual. Then, after these huge meals, he will find himself at an inopportune moment such as this, strapped in to an airplane or in the middle of a meeting in a conference room, with a sudden and undeniable need to go.

Now that he is situated on the hard narrow seat, he takes a look at his surroundings. This is the kind of tight, confining space he never feels he will make it out of alive; the sharp smell of urine and trace of blue sanitized water from the toilet cause his nostrils to pinch. He has to shift his knees at an awkward angle so that his legs will fit between the jutting stainless steel paper dispenser and the opposite wall of the stall.

Theodore often finds himself in situations such as this, in the wrong place at the wrong time, slightly out of phase with the world around him. He should be at the ballroom where his esteemed colleagues are gathering to hear him speak. But instead he is here, contemplating his hairy kneecaps and wondering where in the world his notes might be.

Ilene said she saw them in the room—they must be there. Everything is okay, he will finish here and calmly go upstairs and find them. He envisions them lying on the bedside table next to the clock radio, or perhaps on the desk next to the room service menu and the cunning futuristic lamp. He sees the sheets of paper engulfed in a kind of glow that makes them stand out against the objects around them. They are there, they must be. They contain, in a mere pair of handwritten pages, the accumulated wisdom of the past seven years of his life's work, the most comprehensive and elegant summary of Perturbation Theory imaginable.

A surprisingly rich scent of coffee emanates from the bolus of digested food he has released into the ceramic basin beneath him. Against his doctor's orders, he has once again taken up drinking coffee for breakfast, and he has begun to notice that his excrement somehow retains the smell of it, overpowering all the other ingredients that go into producing this concentrated distillate of his self. This is finished. He wipes himself, stands and pulls up his pants. These furtive movements initiate a startling sudden whoosh behind him. He turns to watch the waste recede into the plumbing on a cascade of fresh blue water and as he does, a series of words that has been etched into the stall catches his eye.

THE WORD IS A LIE

Or, maybe it is THE WORLD IS A LIE, it is hard to tell—there may be an "l" there, squeezed between the "r" and the "d." The graffiti has been casually sketched onto the metal wall with a pen or a knife—or both. There is clearly blue ink in the outlines of the letters, but there is an indistinct mark between the "r" and "d" that makes the message ambiguous.

THE WORD IS A LIE. What does that mean? He looks in the mirror as he washes his hands and considers the face that stares back at him. Dark hair and blue eyes that pale into gray when the weather turns grim. Narrow cheekbones that frame his nose and mouth, and a goatee speckled with blond that Ilene has never really liked, his attempt to look professorial. He would never lie—has never lied. It is outside the realm of possibility for him. His entire life has been dedicated to finding truth, to peeling back layers upon layers of obfuscation and going directly to the most basic reality of human existence. Perhaps he has been set upon this course, this life of fitful lurching in the direction of truth, by an incident that occurred when he was only six years old. He was in first grade, and they had seen fit in his primary school to organize the desks of the students in clusters of four, so that instead of having ranks of students facing straight ahead towards the teacher dispensing her wisdom at the front of the class, the students paid attention mostly to each other. An educator somewhere must have thought this arrangement would lead to a more democratic form of scholarship, students learning from each other, through teamwork and collaboration, but, as Theodore has discovered through his decades in academia since, nearly all knowledge must either be handed down from a more experienced source or painstakingly discovered on one's own. Nearly every committee he has ever been entangled with only served to produce confusion, delay, or outright lies.

Because his desk happened to be the one in the cluster facing the rear of the class, away from the chalkboard and the teacher's desk, he spent nearly the entire first year of school twisted around in his chair, trying to see what the teacher might have to tell him. This arrangement also afforded him the opportunity to stare unabashed at the studious girl with the curly light brown hair whose desk was directly across from him in the cluster. He cannot remember her name. She never spoke a word to him, nor he to her. But she seemed to have something indefinable that he wanted. Then, shortly before Christmas break—they still called it that then—she came to school one day with a milk truck calendar. Now he knew precisely what she had that he wanted. The calendar was fashioned out of creamy beige cardboard, with the name of a local dairy on it, propped upright by a tongue of coarse brown cardboard, and the small rectangular pages of the calendar itself attached to the truck where the milk would have been stored. One day, he found himself in the classroom alone, back from lunch or recess early, and he seized the opportunity to take the calendar into his hands, lift the top of his desk, and stow the calendar in it. It was his now. Then, when the girl came back and discovered that the calendar had gone missing and the kindly teacher asked the classroom full of students if anyone had seen it, he had been forced to confront the fact that he must either confess to taking it or sit there, his face burning with the effort of not saying anything, knowing that the milk truck was parked snugly in his desk, hidden beneath his reading books, erasers, and pencils.

It must have been the next day, or maybe the very same afternoon, when his mother challenged him, inevitably, with his crime. The teacher, as was her right, had searched through the desks of all the students, and had found the calendar in his. When his mother asked him whether he had taken the calendar, he stuck to his baldfaced lie. He will never forget the way his mother dug her fingers into the placid flesh of his upper arm and yanked him, her face as red in anger as his was in shame, pulling him forcibly with her to the car for a trip to the principal's office after school. He has never even come close to telling another lie since that day, nor will he ever.

Entering the corridor where the three elevators are lined in a row, he sees the door to one of them is open, waiting for him, inviting him to ride to his room and gather up his notes. But even as he is letting the door to the bathroom swing shut behind him, the familiar face of Pradeep Malawar appears as if from nowhere, a shadow that has materialized into another obstacle on his path. Pradeep seems just as startled to see Theodore emerging from the washroom as Theodore is to see him. Pradeep's dark face expands into a grimace, hardly seeking to conceal his surprise at finding Theodore here.

"Isn't your presentation at one?" The two of them bump into each other this way so often in the cramped corridors among the cubicles at the Institute, that no other greeting is necessary. Pradeep's office adjoins Theodore's own, and Pradeep will often pop over unannounced and lean his long, lanky frame at a rakish angle against Theodore's bookshelves to bounce a new idea for tackling a research problem off of him or discuss a particularly sticky matter of interdepartmental politics. Sometimes, when Pradeep's feeling playful or wants to get a rise out of him, he calls him Teddy, and it does indeed annoy Theodore to no end.

"It is. I'm on my way now."

"You better get going. I was just by the ballroom and people are already waiting."

How much time do I have? Theodore wonders if he might already be late. A watch would come in handy now—maybe Ilene's was running slow. But he doesn't want to let Pradeep see him sweat. Never let them see how little confidence you have, or how little you know. That has always seemed to be the trick to getting ahead in the academic world, where every sign of weakness, in an argument or a grant proposal or a presentation such as the one he is about to give, will be pounced on and attacked, a point of leverage for someone else to advance their own career.

"I'll see you in there. Are you coming?"

"Wouldn't miss it." Pradeep places his arm around Theodore's shoulders. "Just talk slowly, and take a deep breath now and then. You'll be fine once you get rolling."

"Thanks," he says, and turns to catch the elevator, as the doors are about to close. Pradeep is ten years younger, and some within the department might say that the arc of his career has already eclipsed Theodore's, but there is a certain unrepentant brashness about Pradeep that may disqualify him in the minds of the Board members for the position of Research Director, a job both of them desperately want. The ride is quick, thank God. There are only four floors in this hotel, and their room is four fifteen, an auspicious number—tax day, and also his birthday. The real beginning of spring in the Midwest.

Theodore takes the key card from his sportscoat and slips it into the slot. The light above it blinks red once, then changes to green. Inside the room, it looks as if Ilene's giant suitcase has exploded. The contents she spent so much time carefully folding and packing into its broad bulk have been ejected into the room, extracted and strewn about, her gym shoes on the bed, her blouse from yesterday evening that she wore on the plane, the slip she had on last night at dinner, bras and underpants and a curling iron and a cosmetics bag flung open with eyeliner and mascara and cold cream on the bedside table along with some loose change and a bottle of unsweetened ice tea she bought and the oversized novel she has been reading for about a month flipped open face down to the page she last read this morning before breakfast. Three pairs of jeans laid out at the foot of the bed, remnants no doubt of the decision-making process for what to wear this afternoon to the class and massage.

When he asked her why she had to pack so many things, she told him that she needed to have options, several outfits to choose from that might work, depending on her situation and mood. Magazines about movie stars and their tragic lives on the other bedside table, near the wall, a box of chocolate truffles from the airport newsstand, breath mints, a dinner roll she wrapped in a napkin from the restaurant last night and brought back to the room in her purse, in case she wanted a midnight snack. Three sweaters and two different jackets in case it gets cold. Nylon stockings and four pairs of dress shoes—all of these things she so carefully packed have been unfolded from a state of order into chaos. He sees this mess as if it were that very first explosion that brought forth the universe, the remnants of that initial state of perfect order and unity now unfurled into the infinite variety of states and substances he sees before him. Standing there, scanning the disarray, he pictures his goal of finding a single, unifying theory of everything as nothing more than trying to put all the clothes back in the suitcase, enfolding all the physical remnants of that initial explosion back into a single, unitary point. In two days, when their trip is over, all the clothes and shoes and jackets and toiletry items will go back into the bag, folded up once more into their initial state of order. Everything around him is enfolding and unfolding, from order to chaos and back. His life as a human being is an arc of unfolding from a single cell into a fully grown and developed physical form and then back again into nothing but the constituent parts. Perhaps, he supposes, the original order of the clothes as Ilene packed them in the suitcase still exists somewhere, in a higher dimension, like one of Plato's perfect forms, and the clutter and confusion he sees before him is simply a manifested reality in our dimension, which must always contain the original higher order within it.

He goes to the bedside table where the clock radio stares at him and tries to avoid reading the time—nine minutes until he must be at the podium. He lifts the gossip magazines to see if his notes are there, hiding underneath, where he envisioned them.

No, not there.

Neither are they on the desk next to the room service menu. He picks up dresses and blouses and throws them aside. The notes are not on the bed. He rummages through the remaining contents of the suitcase to see if she might have tossed them in there. He sifts through his small carry-on bag and also his briefcase, the deep central pocket for his laptop and the several zippered pouches where his papers and books are stowed. There are files from the latest staff meeting last week, and correspondence for the faculty evaluation committee he has been elected to chair, but not the two heavily creased pieces of paper he needs most.

The bathroom is just as much of a mess. Both of their toothbrushes are on the sink, along with his shaving kit, four-bladed razor, shaving cream, and a tube of toothpaste squeezed halfway flat. A crusted pale green globule of toothpaste clings to the rim of the sink. Nothing. No sign.

He looks in the closet and in every empty drawer of the bureau where the flat-screen television resides. Maybe he's making too much of this. The outline of his presentation is on the slides on his laptop, already set up in the ballroom an hour ago. Surely he can remember the most important details of what he wants to tell them—this is his life's work. He has something important to say, and he should be able to say it to a room full of two hundred people just as easily as he could discuss it with Pradeep in the coffee shop near the quad. He can remind them that String Theory does not rest on as sound a foundation as most of them would like to believe. They won't want to hear it, but String Theory is only a very good approximation at best, a self-referential mathematic house of cards at worst. Many of his colleagues carry on with their work trying to find the Theory of Everything without realizing that String Theory can only model the universe up to a certain approximation. And the method of achieving this approximation is called Perturbation Theory. It's the underpinning of all the other work his colleagues are doing, yet they conveniently tend to forget it or overlook it. They take it as a given. Pradeep and some of the other young physicists he congregates with sometimes call it Masturbation Theory, when it does occasionally come up in the course of their avid conversations about work—because they think it is a pointless way to waste research time that leads nowhere and can be done all by yourself, over and over again, to infinity.

With String Theory, Theodore knows he can find the answer to nearly every physical question by adding up the sum of an infinite number of terms—this is Perturbation Theory at work. Each of the succeeding terms is smaller than the one before, so he can get a pretty good approximation by calculating the first few terms. However, as Theodore likes to remind his colleagues, there is no proof that String Theory—or the answer it provides to any question—is really complete, or finite, without proving that every single one of the infinite number of terms is finite.

He has always envisioned Perturbation Theory as a long chain of hypothetical numbers, looming large in the foreground and stretching off into the far distance, growing ever smaller as they recede from view. The first three of these large terms have been proven—they are indeed finite. And now, with his years of hard work, he has laid claim to the fourth one, still large and quite important—a vital underpinning to String Theory. But without his notes, will he remember how to tell them that he has proven that this fourth term in Perturbation Theory is finite? Even in his own mind, the intricate series of interlocking equations in his proof seems to shift and squirm, the additional assumptions he has developed to stack on top of the theory and take it to another level seem to evaporate into a kind of hazy mist. Perhaps the missing notes have brought to light his own uneasiness with his accomplishment—perhaps his proof is not really true. He has had Pradeep go over his math time after time, and Pradeep has assured him that it all ties in. The key equations will be there on the screen, projected from his laptop. All he has to do is fill in the background and walk them through how he conducted his research and achieved his proof. But it is all very intricate, and it rests on those slippery new assumptions that may or may not be true. That is what he needs the notes to explain—those notes provide the very core of the research, the hours upon hours of grinding, hard-won logic that separates this work from a speculative grad school thesis.

A pair of Ilene's high-heeled black dress shoes are on the floor—one standing upright and the other tipped over onto its side. Also, he sees now a rubber band on the crisp wrinkled sheets of the bed. No, not a rubber band—it is one of her hair ties, which she used to put her hair up in a ponytail when she went for a run on the treadmill a couple of hours ago, not long after they finished having sex. He cannot understand why she is so driven to exercise. She is a fanatic about it—perhaps it gives her something to relieve the boredom of her days at home alone—but the more she does it, it seems, the broader she gets. Her legs and waist and haunches have grown thick, and he blames the exercise and fad dieting for it. Still, he has remained no less aroused by her presence in bed next to him night after night, in the silky underpants and pajama top she usually wears to sleep. He cannot understand nor have sympathy for those men like him over fifty who require a pill to produce an erection. The slightest glimpse of thigh or curvature of cleavage from most any woman will prod him into a semi-hard state, and he nearly always wakes up with a thick stiffness under the sheets, ready for action. Thankfully, Ilene has matched his ever-growing interest in sex—he wishes she had been as adventurous when they were younger and could do more about it. This morning, for instance, she surprised him by rolling the very same hair tie she would later use to put her hair up at the gym onto *him*, though he was already in good working order—a parlor trick to harden him even more that she must have gleaned from one of her many women's magazines that promise to reveal lists of "Fifteen Things He Thinks About in Bed" and "Seven Steps to Your Best Orgasm Ever."

He is running out of time. There is only one other place his notes could be. There is an outside zippered pocket on his carry-on bag, where he has been known to sometimes stow dirty socks and underwear over the course of a trip, or valuables such as his car keys that he doesn't want to carry through airport security. He circles around to the other side of the bed and is about to unzip the pocket when he hears a high humming sound coming from somewhere behind him. He turns to look, and the humming sound spreads all around him; it is in fact *in him*, like a ringing in his ears. The ringing grows in pitch, higher, exchanging directions from the right side to the left, then back again, modulating into something more than a sound. A vibration has engulfed him, and it merges now with a kind of milky amber light, gathering all about him.

He is not sure what is happening—perhaps he is fainting; perhaps he has passed out and is hallucinating a dream. He is filtering through something that he can only relate to as layers of film. The light and vibration grow more intense as he passes through each layer. The sound that encompasses him is like a pipe organ in a massive cathedral playing every tone at once. And then, as if he has been swallowed by an ultimate layer that is not only around him but inside him, he hears a secret sphere of a voice emerge from the descent within his head, saying *I am, in a word, in an instant,*

and that is perhaps the extent of it,
except for the fact that I go on and on,
forever flooding forward.

This is all inside his head, he cannot see or feel. He has been engulfed by pure sound, the sounding of these words.

Profound the moment when the word came forth
and the crackled sprawl of space and time burst into triumph.
A seed of thought,
a grain of sand that grows and grows,
propelled by nothing more than the authority of my thinking.

The voice is gone, suddenly; the ringing, shuddering noise shrinks and goes away, it folds itself up and the light which is also a part of the vibration lifts away and here he is in the hotel room again. He puts his hand on the bureau at his side, for balance. He looks around him and gathers himself. Perhaps he is going insane. He has never had anything like this happen to him before and doesn't know what it can be. What was that voice inside his head?

The closest thing he has experienced to this was the time twelve years ago when his heart went into a sudden spell of arrhythmia, first racing to an incredible speed, then slowing to a series of spastic and irregular thumps. It sent him outside of himself for a few brief moments, a feeling of being lost within a web of translucent space beyond the normal four dimensions. It had only lasted for a few seconds, this feeling of loosely floating outside his body, and he later reconciled it to a lack of blood or oxygen to his brain. Then, later, after Ilene had insisted that she take him to the Emergency Room and they spent the next few hours trying to get his heart back into a normal rhythm, they transferred him to a regular hospital room overnight for observation, to see if his heart would revert to a regular beat on its own. When it didn't, they were compelled the next morning to shave two patches of his chest hair away and put him under before shocking him with the paddles they always use at moments of desperation on TV, though this had been, they assured him, a controlled and entirely standard way of getting his errant heartbeat back on track.

What they conveniently neglected to tell him until much later, when the doddering cardiologist acknowledged that his heart was in good working order and this episode was probably the result of too many late nights working and too much caffeine, is that his heart would be stopped cold for a few seconds during the electrical shocks they administered. He had, in effect, come back from the dead.

Maybe it is happening again. He puts his hand on his chest and feels his heart beating there trapped within the fragile birdcage of his ribs, slow and steady, faithfully accomplishing its singular mission over and over again, time after time. No, what he just went through was something far beyond a spell of light-headedness. That sound, that voice, had filled him up—it was coming from inside him and all around him at the same time. And he had been transported, as if tunneling *into* himself— down into a higher part of himself somehow.

But he cannot consider it now. He stares again at the clock by the bed and sees that he has only three minutes left. They will all be waiting there for him, the Calistoga Ballroom filled with his esteemed colleagues, wondering where he could be.

Three minutes. Still enough time to make it, if he hurries. But perhaps he should not go, in this state of mind, without his notes. If he tries to wing it, he will make a fool of himself in front of them. He has been apprehensive about this presentation for weeks, and now it has somehow come to this. He could tell them he is ill; he could call Pradeep on his cell and inform him that there has been another episode of arrhythmia. Very plausible, the anxiousness that comes with giving a major speech like this could well bring on another attack. But imagine it: Pradeep, his chief rival for the position of Research Director, going to the podium to announce that Theodore cannot make it, and all of them rising as one to leave the room, the moment of glory Theodore has worked for years to achieve, squandered—gone.

No, he must do it. They are waiting for him.

At the elevators again, Theodore notices that music is being piped in from speakers overhead, lending the hushed vault of the corridor an air of floating, sprightly extremity. Was the music here before, when he came up? If so, he hadn't noticed. Perhaps someone in the hotel has only just now decided to activate the music over the speakers scattered throughout the hotel's public spaces. Or maybe he is only now open to hearing such a sound, after having been filled with sound a few moments before. The music accompanies him as he steps into the elevator for the ride to the ground floor, a pulsating string section dancing on top of mincing triplets of flutes and oboes calling back and forth to one another. He suspects it may be Schubert, one of the symphonies. Theodore enjoys Schubert, but his music seems somehow derivative, a lesser form of Mozart that doesn't quite seem to generate as much of a punch. He wonders whether Schubert would have garnered as much attention without the mystery of his Unfinished Symphony or his early death at the age of thirty-one from complications due to syphilis. Theodore turns this thought around on himself: Perhaps he is too old to accomplish anything great; the great ones, in music, in physics—in most fields—do their best work by the time they turn thirty, and then, if they are lucky, they die, transforming their lives into a dramatic opus commensurate with their art, and heightening the speculation about all the great work they might have done had they lived to a ripe old age. James Dean made three movies. Enough to make him a legend—or perhaps not, had he actually lived to survive them. Jackson Pollock found a tree with his speeding convertible and his mistress in the front seat to save him from growing old with his work. And in one single year, 1905, twenty-six year-old Albert Einstein discovered, in turn, the Special Theory of Relativity, in which he demonstrated that measurements of time and distance vary systematically as any object moves relative to anything else, the quantum theory of light—the idea that light exists as tiny particles called photons—proved that atoms really do exist, added the field theory to the quantum theory of light, and, of course, extended Special Relativity into the proof that matter and energy are one and the same, in the most famous equation ever conceived: $E = mc^2$. And he did all of this while working forty hours a week as a clerk in a patent office, shunned by the cloistered world of academia. What could be more daunting than that set of world-changing insights for any new physicist starting his career, hoping to be the one to discover the single theory that will tie everything together? Theodore is fifty-one years old and is having trouble describing his own little specialized corner of Perturbation Theory. Masturbation Theory, they call it. No wonder.

The languishing string section follows Theodore off the elevator and down the long vault of the passageway that leads towards the conference center. His mind's eye transfers the sound of the vibrating catgut strings of the violins and violas into a set of the subatomic strings that are at the heart of his research. The image he keeps in his head to help him visualize his work emerges—a loop of pure energy plucked by a finger on a hand that materializes from nowhere, the loop of energy twanging in the pattern of a seven-pointed star, a type of harmonics he finds particularly pleasing to envision. Then, he sees this star of light shift to another shape, another pattern of vibration, as the energy poured through it is increased—another pluck of the finger. And this string of light is merely the three-dimensional snapshot of a higher-dimensional object – his mind's eye transposes it as a three-dimensional star-shape collapsing into the vibrating two-dimensional star-string—when, in fact it is really either a ten- or eleven-dimensional energy string passing through the screen of his own limited energy spacetime. But when he keeps his eye focused on the vibrating star of energy and adds others to it, interacting with it, he starts to conjure a swarming field of these vibrating loops and open-ended shoestrings, all buzzing with the excitations of their various levels of energy—and he achieves the fullest sense he can of visualizing the math that goes into creating String Theory. None of this is precisely accurate, but he sees a semi-transparent window of buzzing stars and loops and shoestrings forming into fields of energy that, in turn, interact to create matter, to create objects such as the thick sound-deadening pile of the carpet his shoes are treading on. All of the many things he sees around him, the walls, and comfortable leather-covered chairs, tables, and doors to the many conference rooms lining this corridor are simply half-frozen sheets of energy, slowed down enough to be within the range of his perception as solid objects. And his own research, the subject of the speech he is about to give, is merely the proof that one of the terms in the chain of mathematical equations that describe this gorgeous sea of bustling energy is finite. Because it is finite, in the world of science and math as he knows it, it does indeed exist. What could be more simple?

His vision of that chain of terms in the mathematical equations describing String Theory always appears to him as a sequence of numbers, starting with a very large 1, and continuing on through 2, 3, 4, and beyond, each numeral growing a bit smaller as they stretch out before him into the far distance of the horizon. He has solved for 4, the fourth term—a very important accomplishment. And now, all he has to do is translate this beautiful vision he is holding in his head into words. He must simply fill in the gaps between the bullet points on his presentation slides. But... that phrase carved into the stall of the bathroom crowds into view, supplanting the lovely vibrating strings and the numbers receding into darkness.

THE WORD IS A LIE.

What if everything he is about to tell them is untrue?

It can't be. There are too many wise men who have spent their entire lives documenting, calculating, and expounding upon the theory of the vibrating strings. The gorgeous economy of it—the fact that all the equations describing the forces and particles known to man can be boiled down to the simple condition that strings must take up the least amount of spacetime possible. The mere geometry of strings is enough to explain the way the world works, at least on the flat, two-dimensional level of a chalkboard. But there are doubters. The elegant equations cannot be physically tested, at least with the particle colliders that exist now. There have been beautiful mathematical theories before that ended up proving nothing. And even though the math is lovely on paper, when he tries to project it onto the physical world where he lives, the ever-changing relativistic universe of Einstein, all sorts of infinities and singularities annihilate the beautiful equations. There is something missing—it is like a directional sign, true enough on its own level, but perhaps nothing more than an arrow that points to the real destination far beyond it.

The plaque beside the closed double doors says CALISTOGA BALLROOM. This is it. He pauses, looks down the empty corridor and takes a deep breath, as the piped-in orchestra soars through what must be the crescendo that will tie up all the loose ends Schubert has postulated in the course of his symphony. Judging by the tarantella rhythm and the progression of the harmonics one after another, a sequence of key changes that builds and builds, this is probably his Third. He was only eighteen when he wrote it. It reminds Theodore of a November wind that blows through an Italian forest in the mountains, or a pack of wolves running through the snow. *A seed of thought, a grain of sand that grows and grows.* The voice comes back to him, tangled up with the final drowned out notes of the symphony. *Propelled by nothing more than the authority of my thinking.*

A giant thought that grows and grows. What if the universe is nothing more than that? An idea, pure and simple, taken to its furthest possible extent, from zero to infinity in a single instant. The image flashes before his eyes, blanking out the door and his hand reaching for the handle. A single thought, thought by whom? By someone, the only one, and he is in it. A dream that never ends and never did begin. It cannot be. He is hallucinating, going insane. The door is still here, his fingers grasp the burnished handle and pull it down, which pries the door open with a click and a creak. And beyond the door, as he steps through the threshold, is a room full of people who have been waiting for him.

There is a center aisle, not wide, angled between row upon row of chairs crowded with the most exalted aspirants in the String Theory firmament, which he must navigate. The heads turn, nearly all of them male, many balding or gray, and follow him as he proceeds towards the front of the room where a raised stage has been erected. He can feel the heat of their staring eyes boring into his head. But he does not look at them, he dares not meet the gaze of a single one of them. Each man and woman, every one of them, has done before what he is doing now, has faced a room full of his colleagues and spoken to them of his life's work, boiled down into a few dozen slides and an hour or so of discussion. It hardly seems fair, that this is the format by which his great knowledge, his depth of understanding of the workings of the universe, should have to be transmitted. He would prefer a series of informal talks over a period of about a week in the hallways of the Institute or at the comfortable couches and easy chairs of the coffee shop by the quad. He can picture the windows steaming up there, the soothing smell of roasting coffee lending a magical precision to the conversation. But this artificial division that has been set up in this room, this controlled aura of confrontation between the many, the audience, and himself—the one—is stifling really, a forum for despair.

He spots Pradeep in one of the back rows just past, his eyes inky black. He ignores him. If he looks towards him and catches his eye, he will not be able to go forward. For some time now he has been able to sense in Pradeep a sullen watchfulness, a wariness that is unusual in their exchanges about the daily goings on at the Institute. He knows that it is because they have been rivals now for the Directorship, that Pradeep sees him as his chief obstacle to the next, and most important step on the career ladder. Opportunities like this don't come along very often, and though Pradeep is young, much younger than Theodore, he must know that obtaining a position like that will set him up for life. But there will be other chances for a bright young man like Pradeep. Theodore, on the other hand, is almost past it. If this doesn't happen for him, he figures he may as well resign himself to a rather unsatisfying final twenty years of research on what will likely be increasingly arcane and minor subtopics within the hierarchy of String Theory treasure hunts.

Theodore nimbly dodges the table lodged within the aisle that holds the projector and his laptop. Would it be better to simply turn around and leave now, rather than risk the chance of embarrassing himself by speaking without his notes? A section man in one of his undergrad courses, perhaps one of the humanities requirements he resented having to take, once told him that ninety percent of life is showing up. And he has found this to be true, for the most part, ever since. Show up for all the proper meetings, sign up for all the right grant opportunities, fill out the paperwork, check all the boxes, cite all your sources, and the rest is left to fate.

The front of the room opens before him. There is a gap between the first rank of chairs with their esteemed occupants and the jerryrigged stage, a platform three feet off the floor that he must mount via stairs to the left. He turns towards these and the vision of the universe as nothing more than a thought, the dream of a madman, invades his head again. If this is nothing but a dream, the conception of a giant singular presence, then he can make it do whatever he wants, can he not? For isn't he, with his own tiny glimmer of consciousness, part and parcel of this creation? He can envision himself rising to the occasion, his words lifting with confidence in such a way that his audience will not only be impressed, they will be moved. Perhaps he has indeed been looking at everything the wrong way, carving things apart, dismantling the universe into smaller and smaller pieces as if it were merely a giant machine. The way physics has worked for the past three hundred years, the idea has been that if we could only find our way to the smallest moving parts, we could decipher how the machine works. But that's analogous to trying to figure out what a laptop computer is and what it was made to do by sawing the smallest silicon chip inside it in half, naming it, and declaring that electrical energy flows through it. It's a bit like slicing a horse in two and trying to understand what it is and what it does by picking apart a cross-section of its belly.

These thoughts are distracting him. He must focus. He climbs the three steps, careful now—mustn't trip—and shakes the hand of the moderator for the session, an adjunct prof at the local college, who seems genuinely enthusiastic and excited that Theodore has finally arrived and can now be introduced.

Theodore turns his eyes to the audience, sees only a blurred mass of faces, a carpet of flesh color and earth-toned clothing. His head swims as if the room is in an ocean liner rolling to one side, the sensation of a pool of oily liquid shifting inside his head. He places his hand on the podium for balance.

"And now, ladies and gentlemen. Thanks for your patience." The moderator is a stocky young fellow, Theodore knows the type. Finishing up his thesis for two or three years now, living on cheap food in campus housing, probably with a wife and a kid or two in the cramped apartment with him. Looking forward to rubbing elbows with this crowd for weeks. Lurching towards a desultory future as a prof at a community college somewhere. "It is my great pleasure to introduce to you one of the leading lights in the advancement of String Theory today, a true visionary in our field." Theodore does not begrudge the young man casting himself together with him through the use of the word "our." "Theodore Reveil is the John Stockbridge Fellow at the Institute for Cosmological Physics and one of the founding members of the Assembly of Particle Theorists. He is widely noted for his leadership work with the National Science Foundation and the American Physical Society and has been hailed as one of the true gentlemen in our field." The man's untidy beard trembles a bit as he pronounces these words. "He will be speaking to us today on the topic of his latest research in Perturbation Theory, which will be published in the March issue of *Nature*." And with a mincing step to one side, he yields the stage by saying, "Please welcome Theodore Reveil."

What he didn't expect, what he wasn't prepared for, was quite this elaborate an introduction, and then, from the room full of people who had been waiting for him, a steadily rising round of applause, like a small wave that builds to something faintly menacing as it rolls up on itself and reaches the rocky shore, as if he is not just about to undertake his presentation, but has already completed it. So, at least to this extent, his reputation does precede him. But instead of reassuring him that whatever he has to say next will be accepted by these people as a kind of mildly interesting and enlightening hour of entertainment, the dozens upon dozens of hands beating together, first out of phase in the ragged disjoinder of spontaneous appreciation and then somehow falling for a moment into a kind of syncopated seven-metered rhythm—instead of giving him the confidence to simply launch into his talk (which is titled, as everyone can see projected in foot-tall letters on the screen behind him, FINITE RESOLUTION OF FOURTH-DEGREE PERTURBATION THEORY AND THE CONSEQUENT IMPLICATIONS FOR M THEORY RESEARCH), reminds him of exactly how much is at stake in the delivery of the next several hundred words that will come out of his mouth.

He wonders now what Ilene is doing. She will be blissfully unaware of the plight he is in, having assumed that he of course found his notes upstairs in the room precisely where he must have left them. She will be settling into the chair at her cooking class, in the old house that has been converted into a combination spa, bed and breakfast, and New Age learning center that they passed on their walk through the central city yesterday afternoon, in a neighborhood that alternates between slightly rundown bungalows in need of paint with dusty front yards and the occasional Victorian two-story that has been turned into offices for struggling lawyers or architects. She will be settling herself into the chair with a pleased look on her face, the gentle smile and crinkle around the corners of her eyes that she gets when all the moving pieces of her life have come together into a moment of perfect satisfaction. There will be other middle-aged ladies and young doctors' wives there with her, maybe ten or fifteen altogether, chattering, introducing themselves, looking forward to watching the chef from the bed and breakfast concoct several new dishes they can taste and then try to emulate at home. He wonders if this is perhaps what love is, nothing more than seeing the world through the eyes of another person, sharing the experiences of your life with them, even in imagination, inhabiting their consciousness remotely, and, in turn, wanting them to somehow also see the world as you see it too.

He wishes he were there with her. If this universe were really nothing more than the dream of some sleeping giant consciousness, he could make this afternoon turn out exactly how he wants it to. He could slip out from under the pressure he has loaded on his shoulders, the expectations that live within the heads of the people that sit before him, staring at him, waiting for him to open his mouth and speak. If they are all living within that same being's dream together with him, he is the same as them and can make them think whatever he wants them to think, he can make his words perform whatever magical somersaults of logic and reasoning he has been envisioning now for weeks to suitably impress them. He can be the dream and the dreamer too.

But that is not the world he has been taught to believe in. Since his earliest days he has been told that the world is a place where one action follows another, where cause precedes effect. Where a wheel turns, and a cog in the wheel slips past a cog in an adjacent wheel and makes that next wheel turn another notch. His entire life's work has been predicated on the assumption that he can pry open every living and non-living thing and understand their workings by digging ever deeper, down to the smallest constituent parts, breaking objects into pieces and putting them back together again to generate understanding and knowledge. He has been taught to believe that there is a simple and beautiful language that describes every kind of action and reaction he can observe, expressed by nothing more than numbers and letters and the relationships between them. Everything worth knowing can be boiled down to this—to the kinds of equations that are lodged in his laptop computer, waiting for him to release them onto the screen.

His words and his actions are the only things that matter. He cannot dream an escape from this. His decisions at every point in life are what make his life up, what determine its outcome. And so, he asks himself for guidance now. He has never been a religious man, and he certainly has never prayed, but he asks now for the right words to come, for something deep inside to inspire him. And, to his great surprise, what does come out is this:

"What if the universe, instead of being a giant machine, as we have looked at it and studied it for the past three hundred years, is really a giant thought?"

The words are as startling to him as they appear to be to the people in the front row whose eyes he sees looking back at him. He realizes that even with this first sentence he has betrayed Ilene—who sits blameless in her cooking class in another part of the city, what seems a very great distance away from him—and their future life together, and all the work both she and he have done to get them where they are, but he understands now that it is time for him to begin.

2

"WHY IS IT that the more we discover about the world—the universe—around us, the less we really know about it? We dive deeper and deeper into the realm of subatomic particles, quarks and gluons and leptons, we give these new particles we discover every year strange names and attributes, and yet this added knowledge only seems to underscore how little we really understand. We discover more elements, more galaxies and hot burning stars racing away from us at incredible speeds. We see farther away in space and farther back in time, almost to the very first instant of creation—we can almost touch it—but the final answers always seem to escape us. The nearer we think we are to a final theory, the faster it seems to recede from view, like everything else in the expanding sphere of space. We are continually baffled by the infinities and singularities that keep popping up in our finely-tuned equations."

These words have rushed from his mouth in a torrent of breath, a burst of thoughts that must have been fulminating beneath his day-to-day concerns for months or maybe even years, waiting for this precise opportunity to erupt. As much as he wishes they would stop, they are like an elemental force which, once released, must grow to take up all available space.

"Perhaps we are not seeing with the proper set of eyes. Can it be possible that the very tools we use to view and calculate and measure the world have limited what we are able to see? If we can only prove the existence of one thing in terms of another knowable thing, we might never be able to prove, or even see, what that final thing—the entire thing—is." This is certainly not what he intended to do. He is painting himself into a philosophical corner. No self-respecting scientist in his right mind would launch into a presentation of his career-defining research with a series of open-ended and unanswerable speculations such as this. But the mind moves faster than the tongue. And the words keep coming, trying to catch up. He draws in a gulp of air and speaks again.

"Perhaps this is why we can only ever achieve an approximation of the truth." Now he has found it, the way back, a loose strand in his ramblings that can lead him back towards what he really meant to tell them here today. He dares to look at the people staring up at him. One man in a tasteful gray mock turtle neck sweater meets his gaze with the squinting, screwed up eyes of a bystander who is witnessing a car wreck. "I have spent most of the past decade constructing a set of equations that will yield a result that should satisfy most, if not all, of you here in this room that the fourth term of Perturbation Theory is finite. I believe this is a great accomplishment—it certainly feels that way to me, after a lot of hard work, and false starts, and doubts about whether what I intended to accomplish was even provable. And yet, this is only the fourth term in what is, by definition, an infinite number of terms. A string—if you will pardon the expression—of ever-smaller, more insignificant, numbers that get us ever closer to the certainty of a final theory that works in every corner of the universe. But it will never be finished. Not in my lifetime, nor in yours, nor any other. We can never solve for an infinite number of terms."

Now, though he has succeeded in linking the point of his presentation with his initial febrile preamble, he has also quite nicely succeeded in pointing out the utter futility of his work—and, by implication, the work of all the other fine men and women in the audience, who came here this afternoon in good faith expecting little more than an informative and probably slightly tedious summary of his rather finicky sector of their professional world.

He draws another breath and tries to settle his mind.

If only he had his notes. His hands reach for the podium in front of him. He grasps the smooth wooden edges of it and holds on for a moment. An image flashes into his head, a memory of himself lying on the bed in their old house, the three-bedroom red brick colonial they raised their children in, in the residual waning moments of a hectic, tiring day. His eyes close in memory, and he hears the sound of his teenage son's voice singing in the shower. The words of the song are long forgotten, a lilting pop tune from the late nineties. But the sound, the unrestrained sound of joy coming from the young man's voice, nearly brings a tear to his eye now and he must hold it back and focus. Focus.

His notes—if he had them here, what would they tell him? He can envision them folded over twice, once lengthwise and once crosswise, into quadrants. Two sheets of college-ruled paper filled with his cramped and nearly illegible handwriting. Key equations, the initial building-blocks of his research. And then a brilliant insight, the flash of inspiration that launched him on his way towards discovery: Each term in the theory is a kind of tightening of perspective inward, drawing his viewpoint down to a deeper layer of reality that at the same time expresses a broader and more comprehensive understanding of the universe. And so he built the rest of his research on that insight—it became simple really, years of extrapolation, research grants formalizing the request for funding that would allow him to work out and prove in minute detail a fact that, in his head, he already knew.

He can picture these things, but now he must find the right words to say them.

In the nook beneath the tilted top of the podium there is a digital clock that flashes both the time of day and the duration of his talk. The two numbers read:

1:11

0:00

It does indeed feel as if time has stopped, but it cannot be zero o'clock. It must be one eleven, eleven minutes after one. He must not have pressed the button that starts the duration counter.

These two numbers conspire to mock him. They are both representative of perfect states, a binary on/off expression, 1:11 representing the state where time, and hence the universe, exists, and 0:00 representing the state before, or after, time exists, when there was or will be nothing. All or nothing at all.

The number 1:11 blinks and flashes a new number at him: 1:12.

His son's deep voice comes back to him, haunting, amplified by the years that have passed since that moment and by the pleasing, echoing acoustics of the shower tiles then. Of all the instruments man has fashioned over the centuries, none can match the range of pitch and expression of the human voice. Even a relatively poor singer can create an almost infinite variety of sounds by changing the shape of his throat, his mouth, his tongue, and modulating the flow of air across the vocal cords. And even everyday speaking, as Theodore is attempting to do now, projecting his voice towards the microphone so it can be amplified and carried throughout the wide expanse of this room, is a type of singing, a difference in degree, not in kind. As the next words come out, "During the course of my research," Theodore realizes that he has changed pitch three times. *During the* are on a kind of default middle tone, call it A, and then he goes up a tone to B on the word *course,* not for emphasis, but as a matter of creating interest for the listener. Back down to A for *of* and *my.* Then up again to B on the first syllable of *research,* and dipping down two whole notes to G for the final syllable, *search.*

Re- search. Searching over—and over—again.

All this modulation in one simple opening phrase of a statement.

"During the course of my research," Theodore continues singing, "I have come to think of Perturbation Theory, and, in fact, String Theory in general, as a kind of directional sign that is true, that is entirely valid, in and of itself, but is not our final destination, the final Theory of Everything we really want to achieve. It is an arrow pointing towards a deeper reality, the ultimate truth."

"Where do all the infinities and singularities in our equations come from?" He looks around the room and sees that he has at the very least grabbed their attention, if not their admiration. "Could it be that we are missing something that we are not even capable of seeing, at least with our current way of looking at the world?"

"Could these zeros and lazy eights be telling us something very important that we are simply choosing to ignore?"

He has veered off track once more, away from the comforting set of certainties described by his computer slides. Maybe it would be a good idea to click the remote and display one of those slides on the screen. But another image has entered his head, an image of madness: a disembodied face, an ivory mask floating above a black pool of water, its eyes empty, mouth unsmiling. The mask hovers for a moment over the water and then, what seems to fill Theodore's head, a rustling sound of a wind, a current flowing across the black water as the empty face moves over it. The room before him collapses, the dozens of people and the walls and ceiling and floor collapse; the very substance of time and space have collapsed and there is nothing left before him but a void. A void he must fill. That voice, which called to him inside his head, whose was it? Was it his own?

A grain of sand that grows and grows.

In the next instant, the room is back and all the people with it. Time begins again. And they are watching him as if he never left them.

It is hard to imagine, but quantum theory states that in every second the universe and everything in it essentially disappears and then reappears in a slightly different, changed state—thousands of times. Perhaps he has merely experienced some sensation of this quantum fluctuation, flashing off and then on again.

Nevertheless, they are looking at him, expecting him to speak.

"If the universe really is nothing more than a giant thought, a thought projection emanating from some form of consciousness, and we are living within this projection, it would be impossible to discover the source of this projection by examining the projection itself in finer levels of detail. We cannot find the source of the thought by carving the thought apart, by dissecting it and relating it to itself. We can only find clues, glimpses of the true, underlying reality." The mask hovers over the still black water. "The infinities and singularities in our equations may be telling us that what we are missing is unknowable in terms of physical science. These unsolvable terms in our equations may be roadsigns pointing to consciousness—to God—as the missing piece in the puzzle."

The room has grown very quiet. Only the hush of the ventilation system and the resonating presence of a single syllable his voice has pronounced. It hangs there in the air like the vibration of a giant gong that has been struck, the waves of sound still radiating outward in all directions from their source. He cannot believe it—it seems as if it hasn't really happened—but he knows now that he has crossed a line which he can never step back over again. He has brought God into the equation.

The eyes of the man in the turtle-neck sweater glare at him in disbelief. Others in the front row of chairs are gazing at him as if he has removed his clothes and begun performing a pornographic dance. At the far back of the room, three men arise from their chairs and glance in his direction for a lingering second, then stride towards the double doors, open them, and vacate the room, indignant, letting the doors slam shut behind them with a loud clattering groan. But at least this noise has wiped away the besmirching remnants of that syllable he pronounced, its single vowel sound still loitering in the shape of Theodore's open mouth like a curse he has uttered—G-*aw*-d. It is, in fact, when he considers it, an ugly Germanic word, commenced by the guttural *G*, the mouth opening wide for the *aw* as if in shock or fright, and then clamped shut at the end by the harsh, terminal *d*.

In the murmur that now arises from the audience, the commotion at the back of the room in the wake of the three men leaving, he hears the familiar voice of Pradeep call for quiet. Theodore's eyes scan the crowd to locate him; he was somewhere towards the back. His face is easy enough to find. Its dark skin stands out among the predominately pale pink of the other faces, and when he spots it he sees that Pradeep is motioning with a downward push of his hand for the others sitting near him to remain seated and calm. And he sees also that there is the faintest hint of a smile on Pradeep's face as he does this.

He must begin again. Whatever damage has been done, Theodore must forge ahead with his presentation and complete it. He cannot stop here. If he stops now, the only thing these people will remember from his speech is this blunder he has committed. But if he goes forward and delivers the body of his presentation, gets back to the facts and the figures of it, perhaps he can smooth it over and relegate this unfortunate misstep to nothing more than a shaky start. He clicks the nubby rubber button on the remote control that moves the presentation to the next slide on the screen. It seems almost preposterous to juxtapose the next slide with what he has just said, but there doesn't seem to be any other way back to the safe, orderly world of his research that existed before he began this rambling dissertation into madness. The flash of light on the huge screen behind him, the alteration of patterns and colors and words, does appear to focus the audience again on the front of the room—and on him. So, he can try now to brush this aside. There is an entry point back into the overview of Perturbation Theory that he was planning to use as the introduction to his speech, and he begins his talk again with this: The idea that even though he can never prove every term of the Theory, he can get to the point where the only remaining unknowns are infinitesimal, a negligible variance that he can choose to ignore for all practical purposes. The analogy he uses is simple. Just because a centimeter cannot be carved into slices as fine as the smallest possible slice—the Planck length—doesn't mean that a centimeter does not exist. Once he gets going, the words really start to flow. The knowledge was inside his head all along; how could he have ever believed otherwise? The missing notes do not matter; they were only a crutch he thought he needed. He has lived this research every day of his life for the past seven years, and now that he is on the right track, all the key points begin to build on themselves, one after another, a logical, orderly progression from his initial assumptions right up to the final, crowning equation that appears behind him, taking up the full width of the screen, on slide number 32.

The time has flown by. The digital clock flashes red on the console inside the podium:

1:57

0:00

He has managed to deliver the presentation that he has been envisioning for months, despite the rocky start. Or has he? The clock still mocks him, with its triple zeros. He takes a drink from the glass of water the moderator kindly fetched during the stir and commotion that his invocation of God swept over the room. One last push now, to the finish.

Theodore realizes that he has not really seen the audience for some time; he has been speaking to them and yet apart from them, locked within his own private world. The past forty-five minutes have vanished as he has been absorbed into the concentration and focus required to describe every nuance of his research and mathematical proof. It has been like one of the hours he passes lost in conversation with Pradeep or Victor Fieldman, his mentor at the Institute, in which his mind achieves a momentum of its own that somehow separates itself from the physical structure of the brain and exists, together with these other minds, floating in a nebulous segment of space out *there*—he imagines it in a place up near the ceiling of his office or near one of the chandeliers in this giant room—in an abstract world of its own creation. He has reached the highest point. He thinks of this speech as a kind of symphony he has been conducting. He has led these people through one movement and then another and another, up to the crescendo of his final equation, and now he must bring them down, gently, back to the ground of the real and tangible world. His eyes skim over the crowd of people spread before him, and several pairs of eyes meet his, as if they have been waiting for him to acknowledge that they exist. They seem to be eager to make a connection with him, to show him they have been paying attention to everything he has to say. And then, as his eyes drift towards the back of the room, he sees her. Ilene. She did not go to the cooking class after all—she has been here all along. And even across the wavering expanse of space between the podium where he stands and the chair where she has been sitting, faithfully watching him throughout the past hour, his eyes lock onto hers and he can see what his mind has not allowed him to recognize as he delivered this speech. She must know, sitting in the audience, she must feel it, what he could not let himself understand. The look in her eyes lets him know, as much as she tries to hide it, that he has committed a blunder so terrible their life together will never be the same again.

EVEN THE GRANDEST disappointments and failures are often assuaged by small comforts. After a weekend spent with Ilene together tortured by the saturating presence of his speech, the foggy windows of the coffee shop near campus seem to offer Theodore the first semblance of solace. Finally, away from Ilene, Theodore can for a moment stop thinking about what he has done. Their tour of the local wineries and dinners at high-priced Sonoma restaurants had been purged of enjoyment by the avoidance of the topic most on their minds. They tried to assimilate what the vintners were telling them about the absolute consequence of soil minerals and acidities, grape oxidation, malic acid, tartaric acid, sugars, and how all these factors relate to the taste and "nose" of the liquor they used to douse their sense of doom. But their hearts weren't in it, and each time Ilene tried to reassure Theodore that everything would work out for the best, he knew that she was really trying to convince herself that it couldn't be as bad as she imagined. When he said little or nothing in response, her eyes would dart away from him, look down at the floor or the couple at the next table; anything but see the grim face of the man across from her. They cut the weekend short and took an earlier flight home. Now Theodore feels he can finally exhale, alone with only himself again, back into the routine of a Monday morning on his way to work.

The coffee shop is one of many outlets in a national chain, but that does not diminish its charm in Theodore's eyes. It is wedged among a number of other storefronts on this city street, the doors at the front of the shop opening directly onto the sidewalk, flanked by a dry cleaner and a store that offers orthopaedic appliances—crutches, canes, and other more obscure fittings for bones and joints that no longer function the way they should. The coffee shop bustles with a brisk morning business. A line has formed along the glass counter where fattening pastries and gooey sandwiches are displayed. Recently, the girls who take his order have become more insistent at trying to sell him some of these food items, and he has to tell them "no" more than once—he only wants the cup of coffee with room for lots of heavy cream. They are probably only doing what they have been told as a result of some directive from the corporate offices of the coffee chain, instructing the staff to upsell each customer at least twice at point of purchase. When he reaches the front of the line, he does however add a cellophane packet of dried fruit and nuts to his order, a bit of extra sustenance to get him through this day and whatever it may bring.

A loose crowd of impatient customers jostles near the tiny bar where the drinks are served. As he waits, Theodore's head starts to swim, as if his world is suddenly lurching to the right. He guesses he may be hungry and starts to pull at the taut ends of the packet of nuts. It does not yield at first, and he is forced to pull harder. With an unexpected pop of air, the packet bursts open, strewing the nuts and morsels of dried cranberries across the floor. The woman in front of him looks down at the mess he has made with disdain. Most of the contents remain within the packet in his hand, but it still appears as if there has been an explosion of fruit and nuts that centers directly on him. He stoops down and picks a few of the nuts off the floor, claiming responsibility, but there are too many pieces too widely scattered amongst the wet shoes of his fellow customers to pick up all at once. He stands and searches for a waste basket to deposit the fistful of nuts he has retrieved. The nearest trash can is halfway across the crowded shop, and by the time he turns around again to continue cleaning up the mess, he sees that one of the ever-watchful staff has swooped in with a broom and dustpan to clear it away. He has to give them credit—they do keep the place clean.

His instinct now is to not go back for his cup of coffee, but simply to leave. But when the young woman finishes sweeping up, she hustles around to the back of the counter and brings his drink out, searching for him. He raises his hand in a gesture of guilt more than anything, admitting that he is the one who has caused her the extra work.

"You had the extra large with room?"

He sees now, as she approaches, that he has misjudged. She is not young. It was only an assumption he made based on the type of girl he usually sees behind the counter, and also because of the peculiar hat she is wearing. The hat is a kind of faded velour chapeau suspended atop her head and apparently held in place by a black mesh net that encases it. He seldom sees anything this whimsical on a woman her age. It's surprising that they even let her wear such a thing in this store, it stands in such stark contrast to the green aprons that are required as a uniform.

"I like your hat," is all he can manage to say.

"Thanks," she says, handing him the scalding hot cup. "It's really two hats." With her hands free, she reaches up and tugs the black mesh net away from the underlying tam, which flops down over her ears a bit. "I bought them separately, but then I realized they work better together."

He wants to ask her where one would find such things, imagines this older woman—older than he is—rummaging through bins in bargain basements and the racks of vintage boutiques in the rough and tumble neighborhood that flanks the west end of campus. She must be older than he is. Her eyes have the look of having seen too much. When she examines him more closely, her eyelids droop lower, crinkling at the corners into fine, crêpey folds, as if she is ashamed to be serving him and cleaning up after him. And this is perhaps what evokes the next admission from her: "I just started here over the weekend. The PR firm I was with laid me off... and I need the health insurance." She steps closer. "It's not all bad. The people here are nicer, and I get to listen to this fabulous music all day. At my old office, it was deathly silent. You could hear someone whisper on the telephone from across the room, twenty yards away."

He hadn't expected to have to speak to anyone here. He wants to be alone with his wounds for a few minutes, before facing the day at work. He turns away from her, prying the lid off his cup and pouring thick cream in. To fill the open end of the conversation his mishap has begun, he comments on the music. "Who is this, Bill Evans?"

"Yes." She has followed him to the condiment station where the milk and sugar and napkins can be found. "I think it must be. Listen to those lovely gaps between the notes. The tones just hang there, suspended in the air. He gives them room to breathe. Like he is creating space."

"Do you play?"

She considers. "I used to. I was trained as a classical pianist in college. But I don't have time for it anymore, not the time it deserves. If I tried to play anything now, I'd only disappoint myself."

"I play some," he confesses. "When it's late and no one else is around to hear." He smiles and regards her again. It is a rare moment for him when he can talk to someone about a topic in which he is not the acknowledged expert. He carries so much more around in his head than nearly everyone he meets. "Mostly some of the easier Schubert pieces. I'm working my way up to Beethoven's Emperor and Grieg's A Minor."

"Very impressive—you're teaching yourself? I used to give lessons to the daughters of Hyde Park profs, but I couldn't stand being dreaded so much. And hearing so much bad music. They would look at me like I was running a Nazi death-camp when I made them stumble through their scales. Now I sing, in the choir at the Central Avenue church. Much more satisfying."

There is something challenging about this woman, a sense that she knows how much she has fallen short in life, how many talents she has not fully expressed, but these talents remain hers nonetheless. For a moment, they fall silent and nothing in the store seems to move. Bill Evans has just completed a tricky run up the keyboard and is letting the last note hang in the air, suspended, forsaken. The space between them is only a matter of inches; she is an unstruck tone, a resonance that extends to him and causes him to vibrate at a higher harmonic, like a tuning fork that picks up a sound from the aether. The other people in the store, the hot paper cup he holds in his hand, are merely extensions of the two of them. He turns to take his leave, and the spell is broken.

She calls to him, as he leans his elbow on the door. "If you like music," which she must know by now, "you can come to the church and hear us sing."

He doesn't look back. And as he steps into the frigid February glare on the sidewalk outside the shop, he realizes that he doesn't even know her name.

ON A BETTER day, he might wave to the secretaries that guard the corridor that leads back to his office. There are two of them, and he does think of them as sentries, both young enough to still be mistaken for students when they are walking across campus together after the work day is through. Though their primary jobs are to complete and compile the reams of paperwork generated by the scientists in the warren of cubicles behind them, their most important job is to deflect any visitors who come to this building without notice or an appointment. The work being done here is so highly theoretical that it does not warrant an actual armed guard or any kind of security clearance—it is not as if they are developing weapons systems or the next energy source—all these men are doing is trying to track down the secrets behind how everything that exists came to be. He passes by the two sentinels with his head down, pretending to study the lid of his coffee cup. They watch him pass, and know enough to say nothing.

To his left is the break room, a drab space where he sometimes goes for an afternoon soft drink, a few tables and chairs augmented by vending machines, a refrigerator, microwave oven, and a view of the parking lot. Next to the break room is a small conference room and adjacent to that is the room where the copier, fax, and office supplies can be found. The center corridor he chooses is lined by cubicles, most of them empty, even though he is coming in late today. These cubes are the domain of associate research staff, mostly young men and a few women in their late twenties, some of them still finishing their Ph.D.'s, grinding through the first rugged years of a life spent climbing the highly-politicized ladders of academia. Groping for a suitable thesis topic or research grant, kow-towing to the senior staff members such as himself, whose offices, with real walls and doors and windows, line the outside of the space. By walking down the center corridor, he avoids his senior colleagues in the window offices. He takes a left at the intersection of two corridors in the middle of the large open forest of cubes, and follows this corridor directly to his office, at one corner of the irregularly-shaped building.

He is in. Perhaps the hardest part of the day is behind him, without having to say a word. He lays his computer bag down on the desk and shrugs off his overcoat, hanging it on the coatstand by the door. This is his comfort zone, the place where he does some of his best work, surpassed only by his library at home. Here are his books, his files, his desktop computer, which is linked to the network that shows him the most current results of testing at the particle accelerator twenty-five miles away in the distant countryside beyond the western suburbs of the city. Here are his framed art prints that liven up the plain beige walls and indicate to all who visit him here how erudite his taste in worldly things has become. Here is the sound system that he can use to play his music at a discrete volume, to break up the tomblike silence of the central block of cubicles.

And here is his prized view of the north quad of the campus, with its steeple spires and towers of mellow ivy-covered limestone that climb above the trees. All this is his, and he has earned it. He could close the door if he chooses. He often does for hours at a time, when he wants to be alone with just his thoughts or when he has a daunting round of administrative work to plow through. But that would be too conspicuous just yet. Typically, in the morning, he settles in to the first wave of email and waits for Pradeep to show up. And this appears, against his expectations, to be like any other Monday morning.

    He logs on to his desktop computer, leaving the laptop in its bag. He prefers the laptop, actually, with its clever icons and sleek, artsy design. But the desktop has secure wide-area network access that isn't allowed on laptop machines, and the email loads a tick faster than when he's checking it over the web. There are a couple of notes pertaining to the Board Meeting Wednesday morning, confirming the conference room and meeting time, and another one with the official agenda. This is the meeting he has been waiting for, the one at which the candidates for the position of Research Director will be formally presented to the Institute's Board of Directors, and the one at which, ostensibly, the new Research Director will be chosen. Until this weekend, he has been expected to have the inside track for the job. Now, he's not so sure. The question he has been turning over and over in his head all weekend long is not an easy one to answer: Can a lifetime of laudable work be wiped away by one unfortunate introduction to a speech?

    There are a half dozen more routine emails having to do with administrative matters—committee meetings and reports and communications from junior staffers who tend to copy him on everything they do, to show him they are working hard. He deletes them. If he read all this stuff, he'd never get anything done. And there is another fairly interesting note from Pradeep about the new research they are working on together, a project they are just getting underway on solid-state and fluid thermodynamics that has been occupying most of his creative thinking lately, even though it is a much more applied type of research than he is accustomed to doing. He always likes the startup phase of a project best, the time when all the critical conceptual thinking takes place—framing the problem, shaping the nature of the solution—figuring things out. Other than these notes, there's nothing to indicate anything unusual has happened. Nothing from Victor, his boss. Nothing from Pradeep. No scathing backlash from the three men who walked out of the room, or any of his other colleagues at the Institute. Nothing whatsoever.

Perhaps he has been blowing it all out of proportion.

Because he has tensed himself in expectation of a backlash this morning, he still cannot settle himself into his typical Monday morning mindset. He has a million things to do, only a few of which really matter, yet he cannot determine what to do next. On the wall that faces his desk, there is a framed art print of Degas dancers, the one with the mirror in the middle of the room, reflecting the exposed back of the plump dancer pointing her toes down and curling her foot. Theodore loves that foot—he can stare at it in its silvery slipper, the ankle wrapped by a white satin strap, for great stretches of time when he is lost in thought, daydreaming, waiting for the moment of insight to arrive. Usually, Pradeep will have appeared in his doorway by now, checking in to rehash the weekend and what's coming up in the day ahead, sometimes boring him with a recap of an absurdly drawn-out innings from an English or Indian cricket match he has watched on satellite television the night before. But he has not shown up today. Perhaps this is Theodore's first true indication that things have changed in the aftermath of his speech. Pradeep is the supplicant, who comes to Theodore's office for their daily talks, seeking wisdom from an older and wiser man. The seekers of wisdom always journey to the oracle; the oracle never travels to them. But today, Theodore cannot wait for Pradeep to appear. He must know what the reaction is to what he has said and done—he decides to get up and go to Pradeep's office, two doors down.

Theodore has been mentally bracing for this moment to such an extent that the sight of Pradeep sitting at his desk catches him off guard. "What is it, Pradeep—what's wrong?" He cannot be sure, but Pradeep's eyes have the blurred look that suggests he may have been crying.

"Ah, it is a... an unfortunate thing has happened. My brother," he says, looking away towards the faint winter sunlight in the quad. "His wife is in the hospital, and he needs me to come to Pennsylvania, to help him look after the kids while he tends to her." Pradeep cannot look at Theodore, so it is hard to tell whether he is upset about having to leave town, or something more. "She had pain, sharp pain, in the lower back. And when he took her in yesterday, they found a large tumor. They are operating now." His dark eyes shift to look at Theodore directly, the whites of them glimmering, wet. "They will know later this morning, whether they caught it too late."

The way he has expressed this is typical of Pradeep—minimal, yet precise. The full meaning is there in a handful of words.

"How old are his kids?" Already, they have become his brother's kids alone; perhaps they will not have a mother soon. Theodore asks this question as a way of shifting the topic incrementally away from the chief concern, ratcheting back one notch towards practical matters and the effect this will have on Pradeep. "Maybe Julie can go." Julie is Pradeep's wife. In stating this, he lets Pradeep know that he understands Pradeep is torn by the idea of having to leave town at a critical time, on the eve of the Board Meeting.

"I have to go. My brother asked me." Saying this, Pradeep brings his eyes back to peer at Theodore, slowly, deliberately judging his reaction, and, what Theodore can't help but think, given the situation the two of them are enduring this week, sizing him up, his competitor, his adversary. An opponent brusquely shaking hands at the middle of a playing field before the silver coin is tossed in the air and the contest begins. Then, Theodore sees that something else is enfolded within the numb, forthright expectancy of Pradeep's glaring eyes.

"One night, when I was a boy, fifteen years old, my father died." The words are flat, toneless, recited as if Pradeep were reading them from a teleprompter. "Because I was the oldest son, I had to be the chief mourner, the one who was responsible for preparing his body for cremation." He sucks in a breath, so more words can come out. "I did what they told me to do, placed him on the floor with his head pointing south, lit the oil lamp and placed it next to him. I touched him only enough to move him, into the proper position, as the ritual requires; facing south, the direction of the dead." He blinks once and keeps his eyes closed for a moment, either shutting out a vision or shielding it from expression, so it will not come out as words.

"I had to walk to the center of the village, where the well was, to fetch two buckets of water so that I could bathe his body. When I got to the well, the whole village was silent. It was pitch dark, after midnight. The kind of darkness we never have here, in the city. When I looked into the well, the water black and still, there were two brilliant stars reflected in it, their white light shining back at me from the surface of the deep water." His eyes blink again, once, twice. "And then I saw something else that frightened me: my own young face staring back at me, framed by the two stars in the depths of the water and in the sky above." Theodore is struck by the ghostly image Pradeep is describing, an echo of the white mask he envisioned floating above a black pool during his speech.

"What frightened me then, and still does, was the feeling that entered my head that I was utterly alone. There was no one else but me and those two stars, whose light had traveled hundreds of millions of miles to reflect off that water into my eyes." Theodore can see too, in his own mind, the faint, twinkling light of those stars, so far away, so separate from each other and from the one who saw them, alone on a cold distant planet hurtling through the void. "My father was gone. And I had the feeling that there was only me, I was the only one who ever existed, and everything else in the world might vanish if I were to close my eyes or look away for a moment." His face, turning now to stare at Theodore, reveals that the Board Meeting has been the least of his concerns; his lower lip, drawn back between his teeth, his chin pulled up to keep the emotions inside.

"It was then that I decided, or at least first had the idea, that I wanted to understand what those stars were and how they came to be. I would study them and know what my place was, what my relationship is to them. That black emptiness . . . was a challenge to me, to understand it. If I could understand how it all worked, then I would never have to be afraid like that again."

There is something Theodore wants to say to him, but it is probably not the right time. And, thankfully, he is prevented from speaking by a light rap on the door behind him.

"There you are." It is the administrative assistant of Victor Fieldman, their boss, the Research Director both of them are seeking to replace. She is speaking to Theodore, not Pradeep. "Victor has been looking for you. I came by your office earlier, and you weren't there. He'd like to talk to you now."

So, his sense of impending doom this morning has not been without reason. He wheels around to follow her out of Pradeep's office, and, as he turns to go, he hears Pradeep call after him.

"Ted," he says in a diminished voice, the look of dismay that has haunted him still shrouding his features. "Remember—there is no God."

HE HAS OFTEN followed Amanda through her undersized office, past her desk and the two chairs with magazines arranged on a low table which constitute a cramped waiting room for those who have an appointment with Dr. Victor Fieldman. Unlike most others, he rarely has to wait to see him—and today is no exception. Amanda's sandy brown hair is done up in a loose bun clamped to the back of her head with a many-pronged tortoiseshell comb from which long loopy strands have come free. She is at an indeterminate age that could be twenty-eight or could be verging on forty, an age in which her status as a single woman emanates from her as a whiff of desperation. Her hips are too wide for her shoulders somehow. Her dangly earrings are designed to draw the eye up and away from her body. She is bright enough to navigate the politics of the office and at least recognize at a surface level the topics of the meetings she has to schedule. And she is astute enough to skillfully read Victor Fieldman's moods, an art that took Theodore many years to master.

This is the first time he has ever seen her open Victor's door without knocking; she simply turns the knob and motions him in.

Victor's office is a long, narrow room, unusual in its size and length for this office building, positioned as it is at the vertex of one of the irregular angles overlooking the north quad of the campus. Both walls of the cloistered space are lined with towering bookshelves, two lines of perspective that pull him towards the far end of the room, where Victor crouches behind the hulking mass of his desk. A series of high, lozenge-shaped windows on the left wall above the bookshelves is darkened by blinds drawn tight to disallow the sun from casting any shadows. It could be nine o'clock at night in here.

Theodore has lately been picturing in his head a number of ways he could redesign this office, to make it his own. It is another one of his favorite thought projects, an enjoyable way to while away the last lazy forty-five minutes before five o'clock arrives and it is late enough to venture out of his own office for the hour-long drive home. He would remove a lot of these books and clear out most of the bookshelves; open the place up a bit. Maybe add more comfortable furniture, possibly a couch where he could lie back and think—he does some of his best thinking at home in his study when he lies down and closes his eyes for a few minutes, something he can't presently do here in the office. And also, add several more pieces of framed artwork—he has been spending an occasional lunch break recently at a frame shop in the gritty neighborhood west of campus, eyeing the art prints and European advertising posters they sell there, savoring the process of choosing exactly which ones he will invest in to liven up this room. Another thing would be to take the blinds off these windows and let in some light here— why Victor insists on spending his days shuttered in darkness has always been beyond him. He could do away with the blinds altogether. The slanting rays of sun would make a stunning effect against his new prints lined up on the opposite wall, a kind of art gallery where his own appreciation of beauty can be on display for the many visitors he will receive and entertain here.

That has been the plan, at least, until a couple of days ago.

Victor raises himself to his full height, which isn't so much, and Theodore sees now why he was hunched over: in his left hand he has one of his stumpy cigars he likes to puff on, the lit end of it glowing in the gloom.

"I have to hide it from her," he says, his bushy eyebrows pinching together, like two timid furry animals scurrying to meet each other. "She pretends she doesn't know, but if she sees me, she gets a little mad and tells me to put it out. Rules are rules, you know." He motions for Theodore to come over and sit down, in one of the leather chairs opposite his desk. "I don't like to get her upset." He nods his head vigorously as Theodore sits. "She does a nice job for me."

Theodore agrees with him. "She's excellent." Theodore has been hoping that Amanda will remain on board during the transition period, providing some much-needed continuity and helping him get up to speed with the day-to-day routine of Victor's job. All of these things he has been planning, rehearsing, in preparation for what he has hoped would be nothing more than a formality: the Board Meeting on Wednesday, when he will be voted in as the new Research Director. All of these things that may turn out to be only a fantasy.

"So," Victor says, waving the cigar at him, sending coils of fragrant smoke into the dusky air above his head. "Tell me what this is about."

Theodore doesn't know what to say, even though he has churned it over in his head throughout the past weekend and on the plane home and late into Sunday night, when the jet lag coming back from the West Coast kept him up much later than normal. He knew he would have to speak to Victor about it sooner or later—probably this morning. And here he is, facing the man who has treated him more like a son than anything else throughout the bulk of his career, encouraging him, guiding him, grooming him to be the next leader of this organization. The man who has placed his trust in him. What is there to say? Nothing more than the truth.

"I lost my notes." He starts with this, for in his mind this is still the chief cause he has been able to attribute to the words he spoke. "I was all set to go, talking to Ilene in the lobby of the hotel, and then I thought—shit, where the hell are my notes." He tells it like a rueful joke, something that might be funny, if it had happened to someone else. "So I go up to the room and rummage around, look in my briefcase, under the bed—everywhere. No notes." He runs his hand across his forehead, around the side of his face and down the back of his neck, wincing to remember it. "It threw me off my game, Vic. I don't know how else to explain it. I panicked. You know how it is, before a big speech, you get a little nervous, and then I felt like I was running late, without my notes, and I started rushing down to the ballroom—I saw Pradeep in the hallway, he helped calm me down." He has to get this in, even though it's a bit out of sequence, just to let him know that he always is a good team player. And to let him know that he's not even remotely threatened by Pradeep. Pradeep is still his junior.

"So I get up to the podium, the guy introduces me, and the room is full—I didn't expect such a big crowd, you know, for a talk on Perturbation Theory. But I guess they did want to hear *me*." He shakes his head, thinking about the feeling of dread he had as the grad student introduced him with that long, fawning introduction.

Victor takes a puff of his cigar, the smell of it reaching out to Theodore, encircling him in a kind of dry, acrid web of smoke, scraping against his throat. Victor's eyes always seem watery to Theodore, as if he has seen so much of the universe, he is saddened by how much there is to know. His eyes are pinned to Theodore's words, as they travel through the smoke, trying to evaluate and understand.

"You panicked."

"Yes."

"You started talking before you started thinking. Just to talk." He says this like he's seen it all before. He has seen nearly everything before.

"I did have an introduction all planned out—very smooth. I was going to lead them into the idea of a chain of knowing, how we can get from the fourth term all the way to infinity without losing the continuity of our framework. But that got twisted around in my head, or on my tongue, without the notes." As he says this, he knows he hasn't told him the entire story. He has skipped over that little incident that happened in the hotel room where he heard the voice and sort of blacked out, or something, for a moment. But he has in his mind lumped that in with the general sense of panic, one of the symptoms of simply being overwhelmed by the moment.

"And then it just came out. It was something I had been thinking about a couple weeks ago—who knows where these thoughts come from. You know, I was lying down in the study at home, and I had the idea—it just came into my head—what if the universe is a giant thought? Instead of a machine." He looks at Victor to gauge his reaction. Maybe saying exactly what he said on the stage is not such a good idea.

"You said this, in front of all those people."

"Yes."

"And what else."

"I said—" he hesitates now, thinking perhaps he can paraphrase it in some way that will make this less offensive. But his mind works on it for a moment, and there isn't really another way. "I said maybe—maybe—God is the missing piece in reaching a final theory."

Victor closes his eyes and scrunches them shut tight, wincing. Theodore knows Victor has already heard about what happened in Santa Rosa, but he has not known what to expect from him here in the immediate aftermath. He has not been able to calculate how big the damage will be—he has swung from one extreme to the other in his envisioning of it; everything from a mild slap on the wrist to being fired on the spot.

When Victor opens his eyes again, they are more blurred and dark than ever. He jabs his cigar in the air, which sends a plume of ashes sailing across his desk. "Jesus Christ Teddy. Did you not even have the wherewithal to at least just shut up when something like this crossed your mind? I mean, come on. You can't go around saying things like this. Maybe in the coffee shop or the cafeteria with Pradeep the two of you can carry on with speculating about this and that, or maybe here in the office with me we can have a discussion about whether God exists or not. But to go into a big meeting like that and stand there as a representative of this Institute and talk about God being part of a final theory . . ."

His words evaporate, carried up to the ceiling high above them along with the smoke he exhales.

A part of Theodore's mind has expanded now beyond the current moment. The mind can adjust itself to any new circumstance surprisingly easily, no matter how dire or dreadful. It must. It must go on perceiving, assembling sensations into thoughts and feelings, calculating its next move. This was supposed to be his office, the art prints he picked out were going to be hung on these very walls; but now, perhaps not. Now, a new possibility must be entertained. And the only direction Theodore can come to now is the way in which his mind has been trained over the years, a groove that has been worn into his thinking: He has an impulse to engage Victor in a discussion of the idea.

"Haven't you ever thought of it that way?"

Victor had not been thinking along these lines. He puts the cigar in his mouth and puffs on it for a moment, considering. The question at least seems to merit an answer from him.

"I find it unnecessary to attribute the universe we can observe to a God—a being—man has made in his own image. Vengeful. Obstinate. Wrathful. There is no need for it, and no evidence to support it. If it makes you feel better to think about it that way, fine. But don't bring this Institute into disrepute because of it."

Theodore knows he should quit while he is behind. But part of him wants to at least explain, if not necessarily defend, the idea that came to him at that moment on the podium. The old habits of intellectual debate die hard.

"I understand, Vic—I know I was wrong to say it. Hell, I'm not even saying I believe in anything like that. Like I said, it was just an idea that came to me in that moment . . . of panic. Based on something I was daydreaming about a few weeks ago. It was just a kind of 'What If?' moment. You know, that's how we need to think about things—or at least I do—if we are going to move things forward. We can't be afraid to ask ourselves any kind of question." He can see that Victor is following along, tracking his thoughts. "Haven't you ever wondered, why there is anything, as opposed to nothing at all?"

"That's a pointless question," he says, tapping the ash from the cigar into a ceramic bowl painted with a vivid African design. "Since there very clearly *is* something. Our job is to figure out how it came to be the way it is. Leave the philosophizing to the priests and the rabbis, and the . . . philosophers. As scientists, we can only go by observable, testable data. Not irrational thoughts or feelings. Or a vision that pops into your head."

He has to argue this, he can't let it go. "But what about this, Vic—what if we are not allowing ourselves to see all the data that's out there, because it doesn't fit our conceptions of what is knowable. Or measureable. Maybe we *can't* see everything that will give us the answers we need using our five senses—mainly our eyes and ears—and the instruments that our hands and minds can fashion."

"As a physicist, I hope that is not the case." Victor sighs and emits a nebulous halo of smoke which curls and encircles his head. "I know that we tend to underestimate the distance to be traveled before we reach a Final Theory. But, as a physicist, I *have* to believe that it is attainable. I have to believe that the

Large Hadron Collider will get us very close to the answers we need." He stares at Theodore, as if he is unsure of who he might be, how he got into his office. "And if you don't believe that as well, perhaps you're not the right man to take over the job of leading this Institute."

Theodore knows he has crossed the line yet again. He needs to back off now.

"I'm sorry, Vic. I know I was wrong. You know me—I have to push it to the limit, and sometimes I get in trouble for that. Would you want someone who didn't ask the hard questions running this place? Would you want someone who always thinks inside the box?" He knows he has nothing to lose now. He looks around at the office, the windows high above them, which could have been his. "It's just that, through the course of history, every time we think we're ninety-nine percent of the way to knowing all there is to know, someone comes up with a radical new way of looking at things, and all the old received wisdom is proven to be a hundred percent wrong."

"That's fine—I understand that too. But you were totally out of line in California, and we can go round and round about these things all day, but the bottom line is, you put me and the Institute in a very bad light. I've supported you from the very beginning. And I've been the one who was setting things up for the vote on Wednesday to go a certain way. And now you repay me by doing something like this?" He stubs the cigar out, jabbing it into the bottom of the African bowl. "No more talk—enough." He pulls a piece of paper from underneath a book and slides it across the desk.

"This is a letter of retraction we have drafted for you, which we will publish in the next issue of *Physical Science Journal*. Take it home and read it over. If you want to keep your job here, you must sign this letter and have it back to me first thing tomorrow morning."

Theodore holds the sheet of paper in his hand and glances through it. Certain words jump out at him: *misspoke, misunderstanding, metaphor,* and also *use of the word God.* He feels his face tense into a frown.

"You need to sign this, Ted. Your career is on the line. And even signing this, I can't make any guarantees. I'm doing what I can. I think I can make sure you keep your job, and that's a lot. You can stay on board, continue with the Plasma Dynamics research you and Pradeep have started. Keep your head low for a while and let this blow over."

What he doesn't say, but is evident in his remark, is that the Directorship is out of the question. He can continue with the Plasma Dynamics research because Pradeep will be busy taking over leadership of the Institute.

Theodore closes his eyes and lets his head fall back. He takes a deep breath and leans back in the chair. Of course, it was to be expected. How could it have been any other way?

He knows there is nothing for him to do but sign this. If he signs it, he can continue working, keep his house and some semblance of the life he and Ilene have come to know. He should be thankful he isn't being fired on the spot.

"I'll sign it." He opens his eyes and looks at Victor again. "I'm sorry, Vic. I'm sorry I put you in a tough situation."

Victor folds his hands on his belly. The most distasteful task he has to do today is done.

Theodore takes the paper and stands. And as he does so, his mind turns back to the question that has been haunting him. He looks at Victor and decides to ask him one more time.

"Even if we do eventually come up with a final Theory of Everything, that tells us exactly how it all works, there is one question science will never be able to answer."

Victor stares at him, his sad eyes wide and unyielding, waiting for him to speak.

"Why?" Theodore says. "Why is there anything, as opposed to nothing at all?"

ANOTHER WAY OF looking at things eventually presents itself to Theodore, later that evening, as he takes his seat in one of the balcony boxes at the theater where the symphony orchestra is about to begin: He should be thankful that he *has* anything at all. Ilene is settling herself into the seat next to him, a plush velveteen-covered chair with tapioca-yellow arms that are carved and burnished with golden filigree. The symphony is one of their rare nights out together, an infrequent indulgence along with an occasional restaurant dinner or student recital at the university music hall. The long gaps between these nocturnal adventures into the heart of the city are more a sign of the satisfaction that exists within their lives at home than a constraint applied by their finances. At the beginning of each season, a schedule of performances arrives in the mail, and the two of them consult the calendar to select three or four concerts they will plan to attend. It had seemed to be a good omen that Theodore's all-time favorite piece, Grieg's *Piano Concerto in A Minor*, was scheduled just two days before the Board Meeting at which he would be named to the position of Research Director, and they had both been looking forward to this evening as a kind of laudatory prelude to a week of celebration.

Now, the idea that he might not even be able to treat himself to an event such as this looms before him like the empty chasm of air beyond the railing of the balcony. He pictures himself stuck at home with a stack of high school physics papers to grade, or, worse, slogging through the evening shift at the supermarket, suffering the ignominy of bagging groceries for their more well-to-do neighbors. There are different levels of anguish and pain. He has not told Ilene yet about the letter Victor gave him to sign. He assured her when he arrived home from work that everything would be okay—he had talked to Victor and his job was secure. That was all she needed to know for the moment. He didn't want to spoil their night out with too many details—let her enjoy it. And he wanted to be able to sit here in their box, alone together with her one last time as someone who might still have a chance to do something important, something that might change the world forever.

The soloist for this evening's performance strides onto the stage to the applause of the conductor and the sixteen hundred people in the audience. What always amazes Theodore is how a soloist can simply walk up to the piano and nod at the conductor and then immediately begin striking the keys with such force and control and precision. To the soloist, it must almost be as natural and thoughtless as breathing. The conductor nods back, raises his arms high in the air . . . and then drops them. A long rumbling roll of the tympani sends a delicious thrill up Theodore's spine as the soloist bangs out the first block chords of the piece, falling down the scale into a series of triplets, then gliding back up the keys again in a protracted ornamental run to introduce the theme. The music has the chilling crispness of icicles melting in the dim Norwegian sun, a pristine stream of notes that trickle past, underwoven by oboes and strings. There is a grandeur to this music that has always spoken to Theodore—the trumpets calling out their staccato punctuating rhythms to interrupt now and then the flowing melody that this rather stocky young woman is eliciting from the keys. The soloist must not be much older than twenty-five—a prodigy, a full lifetime of making beautiful music ahead of her. The lonely job of a solo performer such as this in a way reminds Theodore of the work he himself does, the hours of secluded repetition, the hard-fought process of bringing ideas to life. But this young woman must be able to crystalize all of her efforts into a twenty- or thirty-minute performance in front of an audience that is ten times as large as the one in that ballroom in California. What kind of stage fright must someone like her overcome?

After the churning bombast of the opening movement, the performers have now settled in to the quiet contemplation of the middle section of the piece. This is probably the easiest portion to play; a sequence of evenly-spaced chords that transpose the powerful A minor theme into the soothing key of D flat major. This is the part that Theodore should probably try to learn first, but he is attracted more to the third movement, the soaring finish that also happens to be the most technically difficult. He has spent the better part of the past year slowly adding to the number of phrases he can at least play correctly, if not proficiently and in time. Every time he attempts to play it, it comes out sounding awkward and forced—and nothing like what he is hearing tonight. But it does provide him with the enormous benefit of understanding exactly how splendid this young woman's talent really is. Theodore is now witnessing something only perhaps a few dozen people on earth can actually do.

He looks over at Ilene, and it appears that she is enjoying herself. She enjoys these evenings out with him, but he knows that she doesn't appreciate the music the same way he does, doesn't comprehend the structure and meaning behind the phrasing and harmonies that are evolving within the piece as it moves from one strain to the next. She treats this as another type of indulgence of him, his eccentric tastes and habits. If it were up to her they would go to the 17-screen cineplex at the far end of the strip mall down the road from their suburban home and watch a romantic comedy about a woman and a man who love each other but won't allow themselves to admit it until a series of progressively more absurd and embarrassing incidents forces them into the realization that they were meant for each other all along and forever. If it were up to her they would never buy a piece of original artwork. Her tastes are simple, mundane, yet that is part of what he has always loved about her—she is an earthbound counterweight to his speculative flights of fancy. She watches daytime television shows about cooking and Lifetime original movies about women who are drawn to handsome, dangerous men who abuse them. And she loves the modest split-level home his earnings have bought them.

Lately, he has been remembering for some reason a day trip they took together when they were very young, married only a year perhaps. He must have still been in graduate school in Indiana, living in the tiny two-bedroom rental house off campus with only their small mutt terrier long-since passed away and their dreams. They went with another grad school couple, not much more than acquaintances really, a guy he knew from one of his classes and his wife, to a small town in the countryside perhaps an hour or two away, where there is a replica Christmas village that sells holiday crafts and blue and gold ornaments and marzipan candies all year round. It must have been in the fall, this trip, for he has a distinct image of walking to the top of a small rise with Ilene's hand in his, the other couple, whose names he has long forgotten, standing next to them beneath an elegant sycamore tree whose leaves had just turned, and looking out over the town squatting down below, with one of its chimneys emitting a twirl of smoke. He has been wondering why this particular moment has popped up in his memory after all these years, so vivid it seems as if it might have happened only yesterday. And he decides now, as the quiet middle movement of the concerto draws itself to a close, that it must have been for him a moment when he could feel the dream spread out before him, when they had it all to live for, their whole lives still ahead— raising children, buying houses, doing work that might someday change the world—all of it was there ahead of him. Even in the past couple of weeks, when he was still anticipating taking over Victor's job, he knew, his subconscious propelled this image up from within, because he knew deep inside that although the Directorship would be a huge leap in salary and status, it wasn't really what he had always dreamed of doing. His dream has always been to discover something that will change the world forever—perhaps even the ultimate discovery, the Theory of Everything. And this job, directing the research of others, no matter how prestigious it might be, is really more administrative than anything else and would signal the end of his quest to change the world with his science.

At least that's how he would like to think of it. Maybe that's just a story he would like to believe because the job he has been aiming for the past nine months, since Victor announced his imminent retirement, is now beyond his reach.

There is a brief pause, as the third movement is about to begin. The soloist takes a deep breath and stretches her fingers, curling and uncurling them discreetly by her lap in preparation for the whirlwind of notes that is to come.

After a subtle overture from the clarinets, the soloist dives into the final movement with a dramatic run up the keyboard and then back down again. Then a sequence of breathtaking dancing notes leads into the string section driving home the main theme. This third movement is the piece of music he most loves—it seems to transpose into sound his vision of what his work might someday ultimately be—generous, grand, and full of heart and meaning—as expansive and finely tuned as the universe itself. From this vantage point in the box high above the stage, he can see the music ebb and flow across the orchestra like a living thing, the lone piano answering the call of the strings, echoing their song back in a starker and more intricate pattern.

There are perhaps fifty or sixty musicians playing in unison here, fifty lines of melody woven together to create a unique vision of reality. Theodore thinks about the minds of each of these musicians focused on their music, each of them playing one part, but all of them contributing to this unified, complex, giant sound that pervades the auditorium. Each line of melody expressed by one of these musicians is a fragment of consciousness. He watches one of the oboe players, a thin, reedy woman with her lips pursed tight; the music that comes out of her horn started with a thought in her head, and ultimately originated as one grand thought in the mind of Grieg, the composer. Grieg first pictured and heard the notes she is playing a hundred and forty years ago.

Now the oboe player has a few measures of rest, as the soloist beats down on the keys to produce a stunning crash of block chords. She sets her oboe down in her lap, lays it across her legs as if she were riding a bus to work and the instrument were nothing more noteworthy than an umbrella on a rainy day. The work she does is magnificent, but to her it is still a job. She plays her part, contributing to and enhancing the whole. She does not have to shine forth like the dramatic, dark-skinned soloist. Perhaps Theodore has always overestimated his own talent—maybe he has always been destined to be more like the oboist, playing her supporting role. Only a chosen few can stand out from the crowd. Only once in a hundred years or more can a man change the course of history through his science. Why should Theodore have imagined that it might have been him?

The very last crescendos are happening now. The final towering runs up and down the scale, with the full orchestra building ever louder and more intensely behind the majestic rhythm of the keys. Now, the trumpets blare their recapitulation of the symphony's main theme, capped off by seven staccato repetitions of a single shimmering chord—but wait. Wait. Wasn't that a wrong note he heard?

It was. It was off—one of the trumpets, one of the notes of that chord was clearly out of key. He heard it; he knows this symphony so well, has listened to it so many times on the sound system at home and in his car, that he knows a wrong note was played, just a half-tone off, a slip of the finger perhaps, one valve of the trumpet left open or not closed. That wrong note has thrown the whole thing off. The spell has been broken, even though the soloist and all the rest of them are still hurtling towards the finish.

He glances over at Ilene to see if she has noticed it too. But, of course, she hasn't. She is still smiling that secret smile to herself, the one she does when she is lost in her thoughts and nothing around her seems to matter. She isn't paying any attention to the details of what's going on. To her, the symphony is just a generally enjoyable experience, another entertainment. It has no meaning in and of itself.

What about the rest—he looks down at the sea of heads below him and they all are staring straight ahead, like a school of fish, a herd of domesticated animals, oblivious and unknowing.

They don't appear to have noticed either. The conductor—yes, he seems to be glancing, or scowling, in the direction of the trumpets, but maybe that is only Theodore's imagination. It was just a brief instant. The conductor's arms are still waving wantonly about his head—up and down they go. With a flourish, he points towards the strings and asks them for more.

Perhaps Theodore has only imagined it. But whether he imagined it or not, even the thought of the wrong note has shattered the unified reality created by all of these musicians playing together. It has ruined the performance for him.

As the soloist and the orchestra come together one last time to play the final triumphant chords, Theodore finds he must look away. He stares down at the program clutched within his hands and tries to ignore the absorbing and resonant beauty of the ultimate notes, and the searing wave of applause that must follow.

AT HOME, IN the bathroom, Ilene undresses and starts brushing her teeth in her underwear. It is one of her habits that doesn't quite annoy him, but is something that doesn't lend itself to enhancing his mood in the moments before they might find themselves in bed together, ready for sex. He could say something to her about it, but that would only serve to expand this minor distraction into an incident that would certainly break the magical spell required for the two of them to come together, and, at worst, escalate into a full-blown argument between them.

At any rate, he isn't in the mood for sex. They would normally top off a night such as this with a congenial session in bed, but Theodore cannot shake the disappointments of this day enough to avoid another disappointment. That sour note from the second trumpet—he knows he heard it—seems to linger in his ears; he can hear it reverberating through the vast concert hall, a momentary rip in the fabric of the symphony that has grown into a chasm.

Ilene can sense his mood. He sees that by the way she leans over the sink to spit out a mouthful of toothpaste. She doesn't glance at him in the mirror as she does this, only looks down at the bowl of the sink. He unbuttons his cuffs and decides this is his chance to break away. He catches her eye in the mirror as she raises up from the sink and splashes water into her mouth to rinse.

"I think I'm going to go downstairs and work."

"Okay." The answer comes back to him as two even, level syllables, both an acknowledgment and an unstated question, the question being, "Why aren't you coming to bed?"

He pats her, twice, on the bottom, with his hand slightly cupped, as lightly as a small child would tamp down sand around the base of a sand castle, a gesture that is enough to convey to her the idea that he still finds her sexy and attractive, it is only his own foul mood that is deterring him.

Relieved from the pressure of the bedroom, he hurries down the stairs before she can gather enough courage to call after him. He holds onto the railing as he turns the corner at the landing, in the dark. Lately, his hip has been bothering him, his left one. A tightness, a twinge of pain, that makes him take the steps after the landing one at a time; my God, he thinks, this must be what it feels like to begin growing old.

His study is all the way across the house, at the end of the back hallway that leads to the garage, as far away from their bedroom as can be. He often stays up later than Ilene, to work—he does some of his best work in the still hours after midnight, when the rest of the world is asleep and he can be alone with his thoughts. This study is his favorite place to think: the sound deadened by plush carpeting, a desk as wide as the two windows that look out onto the garden, two Degas prints flanking it—the one with the pink and green shades displayed most prominently on the wall that's visible as he enters. Also here, the piano he uses to distract himself when the work is not going so well.

The sheet music is open on the stand above the keys, taunting him, luring him. It is more a book than a sheet, the entire Grieg concerto he heard only an hour and a half ago distilled onto 72 pages of paper. The score shows both the piano solo and the orchestral parts below, for reference. From a few feet away, the music appears to be a blur of dots and dashes, a secret code only a madman could read, crazy patterns zig-zagging up and down and across the page. He moves closer, drawn to the silent challenge of the score. Examining the music written out this way always proves to be a bit daunting for him: Look at all the notes, the beams and dots and demi-quavers and crochets, the prickly sharps and flats that litter the runs and transmit the feel of fingers trickling up and down the keys. How could one man conceive of such a thing? And then, having conceived of it, how could he so precisely translate his vision—his audition, more properly—onto the page?

Theodore sits down at the bench before the piano and turns to page 58, where the very last section of the third movement begins—the culminating majesty of the final runs and trumpet blasts and rolling tympani. He rolls his head around, shrugs his shoulders and shakes his hands to loosen up the fingers. He pronates his left foot, to get ready for the pedals—it feels as if he has banged his ankle on something, as if there is a bruise right on the ball of it, one of those odd aches and pains that he sometimes feels without knowing where it has come from. In his head, he hears the woods and strings play their jumping background rhythm that leads directly to the alternating left-hand chords he starts to play as a lead-in to the first trilling runs of this final six-minute section.

It is not all fast, but it *is* intricate. He bangs it out, with feeling, leaning his weight on the keys, bringing all the sound he can out of this little upright piano, pausing for a moment here and there where the orchestra is supposed to echo his runs. He has been working on mastering this section for eight weeks now; he knows he should begin with the slower middle movement, but these 88 bars of music are, to him, the epitome of greatness, the condensation of everything he feels about his own work, expressed in a wall of melody.

The sound is not the same—in his mind he hears the great soloist from a short while ago playing, the huge concert grand, like a giant harp laid down on its side, sending waves of thrilling notes across the giant space of the auditorium. But here, the notes are muffled, muddy, slightly off pitch. The piano needs to be tuned, and its small upright sound board will never match what he heard earlier this evening. A piano like that must cost two or three hundred thousand dollars.

As he attempts a delicate run in which he has to cross over his hands to get all the way up the keyboard, the fingers on his left hand catch, stumble over themselves, and falter.

The notes come to an abrupt stop.

He will probably never learn the entire piece—he will certainly never master it. Better to give it up.

Better to abandon the pursuit of excellence than to keep plodding along in a halting, stumbling, defiantly inferior manner. *Enough.* He will sign the letter, and, in doing so, formally give up the idea that he might ever accomplish anything as masterful and filled with genius as playing a piece such as this, or writing a piece such as this, or discovering a basic principle of the workings of nature. He can finally admit now that he has never possessed the spark of genius required to do these things.

He stands up from the piano and turns to his desk where the letter waits, hidden beneath the portfolio he uses for meeting notes. He reads the entire contents of the letter, standing, his hand quavering a bit as he holds the creamy rag paper Victor's assistant uses for official documents. His eye is drawn to one sentence in particular: *I freely admit that my use of the word "God" in my speech was a deviation from the proposed presentation approved by the Institute for Cosmological Physics and the New International Perspectives on String Theory Symposium and reflects a personal wording choice that was an attempt to provide a suitable metaphor for concepts that often prove difficult to describe outside the realm of mathematics.*

When he considers it carefully, he must admit that all of this is true. He was grasping for a way to express ideas that had been bothering him lately, in the run-up to the conference. And, it is true, that what he said was a deviation from what Victor saw and signed off on before the paper was submitted for publication and the presentation was sent to the conference chair. It's all true, all the mistakes he has made. All the shortcomings.

He lays the paper down on his desk and takes up a pen. He glances at the empty space above his printed name for a moment and then slowly, carefully, draws the pen across the rough texture of the page, making sure each letter of his name is entirely legible, so everyone can see:

Theodore J. Reveil, Ph.D.

There is nothing left to do—he can let go now of everything that has ever mattered to him, of everything that has made him who he is. He goes over to the day bed on the far side of the room and lies down on it, closes his eyes, and lets it all return to its native nothingness.

THE DREAM BEGINS simply enough, as an encounter with his brother, whom he rarely sees these days, down in Texas with his two small children and his happy, conventional life as an insurance adjuster for the frequent weather-related disasters that plague the region, hurricanes and twisters and hailstorms, lightning strikes, fire and brimstone. As is usually the case, there is enough incongruity in the setting to let him know it is a dream. Geoffrey (not Jeffrey, their parents had a penchant for granting their children old-fashioned, more-British names and spellings) enters the living room of a house that feels very much like their great Aunt Irma's house, a house Theodore has not thought about, much less visited, in nearly thirty years. He has in tow both of his young children, Avery, the girl, and Cassidy, the boy. Geoffrey was not going to saddle his own children with conventional names—no, they would have uniquely current names that carry little meaning. And the children, in this dream, are even younger than their current age, maybe three and five. They are happy to see him, their uncle Teddy, and perhaps that's why his mind has placed them all in old Aunt Irma's two-bedroom bungalow, giving extra emphasis to his role as an uncle in that way dreams have of giving us extra perspectives on things—he is in a way seeing the encounter both through his own eyes and through the eyes of the little children, and from above, as if he is floating near the gabled ceiling of the sparsely furnished room, a benign god-like presence overseeing all.

Now he sees that he is holding a large, floppy, leather-bound book in his hands, and as he opens the book to show Geoffrey something in it, his brother comes near, holding little Avery's hand in his, and the three of them read the single line that is printed in the middle of the silky white page: WE ARE EACH OF US BEINGS OF LIGHT.

The words would seem to emit a shimmer of careless energy, transmitting a smile to Geoffrey's face. Theodore turns to him and nods, as if to confirm the validity of the message; always the teacher, always the purveyor of wisdom, always smarter than the rest.

Then, something profoundly disturbing happens. His viewpoint draws within himself for a moment, and then is lifted up, away from this room and any other and, what's more, releases itself entirely from his body. The pages in the book evaporate from view, and the house and people with it. Everything draws itself to a solitary station within him. Everything collapses into nothing, and every thing that made him who he thinks he is is gone completely. He is drawn within and lifted within, he is every reason and no reason at all. He is dressed in nothing, no longer clothed in the body that has carried him, he is beyond that now. He slides within a filament that draws around him like valves releasing him to another world. He sees this as a film of burnished celluloid, a bustling swamp of cells surrounding him, blinking, bunched up verdigris, a swarm of liquid animals that might be his very own.

In a corner of his vision, another layer appears; another and another, drawing him down, within. He passes through several layers and stops, it seems, in one. In this layer the cells are gone and there are only patterns, shapes, relationships. Brightly colored textures, flashing past him, cords of fabric woven from boiling worms of ruling death. Molecules that bind together, attracted one to another, tendrils of particular weight and thickness that dictate whether or not one may happen to link to this one or that. And soon enough he passes through this, drawn down once more past layers upon layers, each more fantastic than the next.

Whatever corner of his soul has opened up to reveal has drawn him down and within to restless wandering, a fitful flight of midnight learning, quenching his true scholarship by means of miracle and glorious scrawled delight. Here nothing seems as it is and the dust of his imperiled intellect has been swept aside, leaving only the essence of matter itself laid bare. The ground of being sweats away a monstrous secret excellence. The ordering of every level makes way for one far deeper and far more intricate than the one last. Wave upon wave of violence operates here and now the final unity of matter shuns the forms he would recognize as his own. Here buzzing particles shimmer and flit by like tides of trembling light. Here hosts of frozen absolute passion form the final layer of something that could leap from one state to the next. Distance, space and time are nothing here—there is no time or space. When only energy is present, in its primal form, its first endeavoring, then only emotion rules the superabundance of power. Time cannot be measured without a gap between one second and the next. Space cannot be measured without a stopping point, where one thing is and another isn't. When all everything smoothly flows throughout, there is no longer here nor there. There can be no yester-day or to-day. There is only the swinging constant rhythm of total lacerating Now.

There is only every covenant of droves of buzzing particles, a shimmering flow through copious proud and angry lust. And finally, when he thinks his head will burst with the staggering pressure building out in all directions, it stops.

It stops, and opens to reveal.

Reveal; now heaven opens in a dream.

Heaven, true to light, a primal empty vastness on beyond whatever lies on top of it, brushed and varnished empty vastness, too enormous to be real. All everlasting nothing opened up to a chasm abyss wider than a sky that held a leaf that fell and landed in a perilous delight. Perhaps a tenuous cloud existed here once, but if it ever did, there can be no trace of it now and here there was no yester-day, is only evermore. There can be only pure fantastic vastness, an emptiness that has no bounds and makes the vacuum of space appear to be a teeming jungle filled to the brim with stuff by comparison. It is a nothingness that supports all the layers he fell through with its serenity and calm. It is a naked gleaming pasture of clarity through which all the other common blooming filth of existence can emanate. It is the single place from which everything ex-ists. It is the unitary moment from which all days take place. It is the one and only thought from which all other thoughts deliver.

It is.

And there can be no other.

It is the roiling surface of the sun scraped smooth until it is only light. It is the proud reluctant vastness of a shore that knows no end. Two cubits and four cubits, four cubits and eight. Flashing screeching something was a beast that meant no harm from fullness of a whim to terrible love or blood must slobber and groan and forge a tabernacle of hosts of tender impatient imagining there goes no other lure no other bait and cast and significant of the wherewithal to turn away from here to preach and keep on preaching to stare into the vastness of a crippled wave of curative disease to harken to the listless tentacles that rip apart a swinging necessity that never goes away.

Yield and never yield, never stand apart and never waste the start of nothing never the savage instrument of his demeanor launching startled flesh-and-bone delight; how many times has this tautology been taunting him and us and them? How many vitriolic modulations terminations terrifying dress and sword and shield and analogy to meanwhile great performance field reveal. In Kepler's tentative abundance of forms and formulations there was naught imperative to which a decaying shadow of doubt were instead of protable sweat and shorn. And shore again and faith who lived for me who knows for him the days and nights that mount to thee the boy that counts the agony. And drift bespoke beside the English passion the daughter raised and honed and silently prepared for slaughter. Wherein there is the giving up of eyes of sense relation between perceptual and untarnished thought secure. Wherefore there is the supper time dilation of a heart's abundant beating. Wherever may come the ruined palaces of long and latent reversible respites. Wherefore the two men who came to love the wretched summits of the earth the hallowed valleys of Copernicus delight, wherefore these two men who came to love were smitten by the very selfsame cause and ceaseless maker who made them. And whosoever triumphed by existence in and out of time harmonious and also riven senseless by fear, whosoever brought the channel of a smell of tinctures and ointments unto the prime and incarnal maker, for whatsoever reason, for whomever could excuse him and shed his chains before the gallows baleful appeal, those are the ones who are nothing but the portals of the maker. Those are the ones whom Newton found in surrogate murmurs of the night. Whenever a half-insistent arc or formula for parabola joins the weather wander for a final peril or venality in spite, whenever terminations of points or lines are proven limitless by bounding up and out to further ever onward other dementias and dimensions, destinies and destinations, whoever sought to lessen the fair finality of expanding outward glow of light by whatever self-wrought frailty or treason, those are the ones whom Andromachus twirled and intertwined and over turned before they could ingratiate themselves before their maker.

And the likeness of the harps and bugle calls is the flaring trumpet of the hymn of all existence flaring out from a single point of nothingness to everything that is like women with sympathy and mourning a hollow firm receptacle for longing, that is what emanates from the suns and moons and stars nothing more than vast and fugitive longing, stretching out and out and out so far curved it tends to straightness, so long-standing it flashes into emptiness and disappears.

Thus were their faces inquired and registered from a form that molds them they leaping go pre-made thoughtful imagining unto light infested swirls of substance coming round romantic glooming together that was just before the sun went down in sad and eager wantful tending to delight; thus were their faces formed their bodies round their famous debris and shattered numerary nights; thus were their likenesses established in manner like the universe itself, tending from one spot to many, from one thought to many; thus were their likenesses the basis of their forms, their images the forms for their bodies through and true.

Moreover he said to him the son of every father who never was go forth into a simile of perfection, go onward from the thought that made you into the wretched indicating stalwart loins again, go you forth into becoming and being in time again though you are merely only a product of my thought; for thought must manifest and ex-press, thought must image make and engender love and life and distress, must press out into some thing and every thing in order to dis-cover what it was that made itself.

And

The likeness

Is a product of

Itself by means of itself and itself alone,

Whithersoever the spirit is to go, there shall every weight and grip of earth and enchantment,

Encompass the breath of spirit, endeavor to unfold within a sheath light slowed down enough to pull together as a bright and insubstantial whirlwind of matter, the first-slung fouling come-together of glory.

Two cubits and four cubits, four cubits and eight, by this means and method does the timeless image turn to light and from light to speck and speck by speck to propagate, by ever furling outward and twisting back upon itself. And they went in ashes swathed and silent to see him staring aghast and in some terror night regime in recompense to flow.

Their wings were rude and scattered joined to vanity and heavenly circuits of the golden orb gymnastic from heath of knowing trestles planks and flowers, sweet flowers plucked from living fire of elemental man and vengeance in and under, down to the bones and solitude of risen nature rising out of furling light. Grow and grow, always out and out and ever onward, burst from single orchid blossom originating thought from imageless ground of being light infusing elemental image imperious, all must always grow. Always on and on, forever outward he is one with it, there is no other one, only a means of reaching out that is fallen back upon itself in this present only moment, and every separate form proceeds from that harkening and sunken urge.

And under the firmament there is no-thing and there is every-thing, all everything exists as a perfect naught a point which realized itself and ex-pressed itself, pressed itself out and unfolded into something and that moment came as one and is even yet be-coming. It spirals out from unity to infinity in a trifling wayward motion. It beckons to itself, and thereby unfolds and flees and turns back within again, immured and formed of pure thought projecting light, which is thought projecting through a seam. Once it has happened, it always will, it always does. Once a proper sweeping through the night of snow flashing brilliant common looking clothed in rich array of supplications, armed in armor unthuswise, singing songs of sacred sweet delight, the terrible and the curving bright apology can never unfulfill what always is. Even as the love and beauty polish and shine the brightness of his sight, an alternate fistful of ashes clouds the common weal, for everything that can exist must exist. Tear apart and rip to shreds the loveliness of a woman's face, drop a tower from the heights into a smoking pit. Violate the bloody mass of guts and bones were broken, gnaw on carnal beasts who give their flesh so other flesh can consummate in potent longing, penetrate a wretched fold of familial fertility so lordly on a languid spurt of sunken down obsession. Wither away the uproarious orgy casting shallow death aside as a form of transposition, silent worms give all their effort into turning us aside.

As an adamant rejection of true sight and knowing, only a slender tube of vision comes to pass, only an incomplete incorporation seen in sequence moment after moment. Alpha and omega exist at once and the first thing is not past, the last thing hurtles outward faster than a man can see. The horizon grows both larger and smaller, as the microscopes and telescopes unveil the magnitude and triviality of what a man can never comprehend. Horror is only embracing what he thought his friends might slight him when they were taken through the crowded world which crowds him down in finite perception, terror only shows him what he could not bear to see. Honor only palls before the wealth of meaner measure than forever, only quails before the protean sweat and tincture of a wound too wide to heal. Onward, on to sweet delight, ever on and ever quite complacent with the weak offending effort that has brought him near enough to know he never will be quite enough to realize the prism of his fractured various reality. No is but the future tense of yes, brought forward through the drafting yesterdays of fortune, for this is the shape of a dream; there is nothing straight about it, only man presumes to make a line that does not turn. Obey my final word there you will see the angels and the sky and afternoons and desperate workmen fisher on the shore a river current heedless wheat and hum of multitudes come up the stair two tables of stone in slowly millions driven tabernacle disembodied you will see the glacial broken father and his holy book and clear and high above you see the rescuer the night in woe the streets that plough the forward trough the fields that pave the proselytes the dark ship hoeing through the night, heed my final word and there you see the reek of stars moving backwards retrograde inspection you see the reeling of the wretched war-workers the hampered diffidence of sex the once dilation the fallings and the yearnings the rift and wrack of comfort in the continents that no longer tip into oceans that swallow them up they have been and always will be swallowed up, hearken to my final word there you will see the riven priest the garden urn the mountain where they both are full of eyes and ashes the forgiven man the daughter who listens and the full applause of fruits and flowers bearing into light the hole the size of nothing the twist of water in a drain the circle caught inside a circle, heed my final word and you will hear and see the tourniquet the old silver walls of barracks fallen in the snow the wisdom cruelty of a man who stopped the road the journey never ends it is an adamant rejection and you will see and hear until you see the yearning portion of the dream that seeks itself you will hear one word which withholds all sound and has quelled the nighttime into day.

HE WAKES. HIS eyes open and he sees that a candle is burning on the table beside the piano, though he does not recall having lit it. From the amount of oil in the trough around the wick, it appears to have been burning for several hours.

What time is it? There is no clock in this room—he hates the sound of a ticking clock, its insistent rhythm urging him to go forward, forward, reminder of another moment of his life wasting away. The grass of the yard that slopes down towards the Heisels' house on the next cul-de-sac over suggests the first insipid shimmering of dawn. The branches of the ash tree waver in the dim half light, stirred by a breeze that carries the treacherous frost of a February morning. But his eyes are filled with what his mind has seen; his head is full of other images. He sits down at his desk and tries to understand. Was it merely a dream, or something more? There seems to have been an otherworldly quality to what has taken place—and that is the key to it: he has not only seen these things, he has heard them and felt them. He was *taken* to another place, outside himself, above, within . . . beyond. He has had a vision of something that, in his mind, feels like a complete and unified whole, a snapshot, in one long, extended click, of everything that is. He closes his eyes again and he can almost see it, a kind of oval ball, in which everything is wrapped up, floating, spinning.

He takes up his pen and opens his notebook and starts writing, whatever comes into his head, his impressions of what he has witnessed. He has to get this down, capture it somehow. He has to convert it into something that he can remember and convey to others:

There is a unity to everything, from the largest forms to the smallest. The spiral spinning of a galaxy is the same form embodied in the twist of light that comprises the most minuscule particles of matter. And the spiral is a two-dimensional slice of the three dimensional form of all matter, which is a torus encompassing the central point of emission. All matter, on the smallest and largest scales, constantly emits from a central singularity and flows out, swirling about the central point in an ellipsoid current which is dragged around and drawn back inward to the central point again, into which it returns to start the cycle ever more. The shape of a tree, and an apple, and a cyclone emulate this outward flowing—the tree flows up from the roots through the trunk and out through the branches. The apple flows up through the core and out at the top where the stem protrudes. The energy that establishes the human form circulates in the same twisting toroid around the spine. And every particle, quark and lepton and gluon that conspires to generate these forms is created by light—pure energy—that twists around a point in various manners, which gives the particles their flavors, their various spins and attractive powers.

This is the shape and manner of the universe, a giant twisting ellipsoid of energy that did not erupt in one big bang, but is constantly bursting forth, at every moment filled with energy, imbued with light and life.

There is no time—it is always happening. There is only the eternal Now. We are tricked into seeing time and space by the limits of our perceptions. We see this infinite happening through the tiny tube of our eyes and ears and can only experience it as a sequential unfolding and enfolding. To us the universe is expanding at an ever-accelerating rate because we cannot measure eternity or infinity. When we create a more powerful telescope or microscope, we're confronted once again with the limits of our own knowing by an ever broader, or more minuscule, horizon. We are not big enough to see it all at once, but we think that whatever we see is all there is, when, in fact, everything outside our little tube of limitation is more than we can ever hope to know. We seek to place our limitations upon the staggering wealth of creation, and then we wonder why we stumble upon mystery after mystery. The universe keeps growing, because there is no end to infinity, we cannot comprehend.

There is no gravity—gravity is only our experience, our measurement of unity, the mere fact that everything is bound together as one. Instead of seeing all things connected, we try to slice them apart, give them separate names, and act as if we know them. When things fall apart and decompose and die, we are only seeing the inward turning back of the flow towards the source from which it came. And we wonder why things must end, when there never is any end.

Once anything exists, it all exists—now. So, anything that can happen, must happen. Is happening. In an infinite and timeless universe, everything that can be imagined exists all at once. We simply can't see it all or experience it at once. So we see time and space unfolding. We see terrible explosions of light and plants and animals growing and dying and stars twinkling across fathomless chasms of darkness. And the shape and form of the universe is a constantly swirling unfurling and enfolding of a giant thought. And nothing is faster than light, because everything is made of light. Everything *is* light. Light is conscious energy, the medium of thought, and thought is all there is, a giant timeless thought.

He raises his hand from the page and sets the pen down.

That is the best he can do, for now. These things he has written don't really make a lot of sense, but it is the closest he can come to describing the things he saw and felt—it was more of a feeling really. If he stops, with eyes closed, and holds it still within a spot in his head that seems to be just above his eyebrows, in the middle of his forehead—there—he has it; if he holds it there for a moment he can feel it again, the feeling of holding everything together in one spot. When he has it there in one place he can see that the man-made scientific theories are not wrong, they are only partially right. Relativity is right, and Quantum Theory is right, and Newton's laws are right, and String Theory is right, and Perturbation Theory is right—they are all accurate and useful ways of describing the universe. They are not wrong and they are not incompatible, they are merely woefully incomplete and limited by their frameworks of knowing. He sees this now, and it excites him to envision these ways of describing the universe as if they are all little tubes he can use to peer at a giant object. It's as if he were to look at the back yard through one of those cardboard tubes that's left over when the paper towels are used up—what he would see through the tube is not *wrong*, but it is only a very limited picture of the great big world and it would only partially fit with what he would see if he were to look through a different size and shape of tube from a different angle. Both of these views through the tube would be correct, in and of themselves, and could prove useful to understanding the world around him, but they would never get him all of the way to seeing a completely accurate and true understanding of everything that is out there.

This idea excites him tremendously—he can picture Newton standing at the kitchen window with his cardboard tube and Einstein at the bedroom window upstairs with his cardboard tube and Heisenberg with his uncertainty principle downstairs at the small basement window peering up through his own tube, and all of them looking at the same giant ash tree rustling in the breeze, and each of them having a true but slightly different view of it. And none of them seeing all of the branches and the trunk together, just their own slices of it that in some parts overlap. Only someone who isn't looking through one of those tubes, who might be standing high up on the hill in the opposite direction of the Heisels' yard would be able to see the whole tree and know precisely what its form is. This is the idea that Theodore is trying to hold in that spot in the middle of his forehead when he sees the entire vision in terms of an equation, a set of symbols that appears before his inner eye. He hesitates for a moment, then writes it in his notebook:

$0 \times \infty = 1$

This makes no sense. There has never been any mathematical system in which the equation he has just written would resolve as a proper solution. He states the equation in word form to see if it makes any more sense: "Zero times infinity equals one." No, still absurd. Still wrong. Zero and infinity cannot be multiplied together. Zero times anything is zero. And infinity cannot be operated on in an equation. Infinity is merely a result that indicates a problem in the math.

He crosses it out. And then he goes to his laptop and starts the email application and creates a new message addressed to himself. He starts typing in the words he just wrote in his notebook—this is the way he sometimes saves his work, his notes. If he's working at home here late at night, he'll send himself an email message that he can open the next morning and copy to a document on his desktop computer in the office. This way, he has the assurance that he has preserved whatever work he has done on the Institute mail server where the email message is stored. The words feel strange to him as he types them into the message, as if they have been sent to him by another person, another version of himself.

There is a unity to everything, from the largest forms to the smallest. The spiral spinning of a galaxy is the same form embodied in the twist of light that comprises the most minuscule particles of matter. And the spiral is a two-dimensional slice of the three dimensional form of all matter, which is a torus encompassing the central point of emission . . .

It doesn't take long to get it all down in the email. A couple of minutes, and he is at the end. He is about to send the message, but he pauses and stares at the strange equation he has written—written and crossed out. It is absurd. But he types it in anyway, searching for the special symbol code for infinity in the equation app the institute has added to the email program for its scientists to use:

$0 \times \infty = 1$

Zero times infinity equals one. Absurd. He stares at it for a moment longer, then clicks the button that says SEND.

3

THE MORNING ARRIVES too soon. He goes to the kitchen and dumps a filter and coffee grounds into the coffee-maker, fills it with water. Already, the light is gaining strength—the digital clock on the coffee machine says 6:23, the ones on the microwave and stove say 6:24. No point in trying to go back to sleep now.

Dragging up the stairs, Theodore steps over the third step from the top, the one that yields a loud, groaning creak every time it is stepped on coming *up* the stairs. He skips the step and hangs on to the rail in order to avoid waking Ilene. At this hour almost any sound will be enough to wake her. And if he wakes her now she won't be able to go back to sleep.

Gently, gently, he turns the knob on the bedroom door. It too makes a kind of clunking tumble of loose hardware from within the mechanism that he knows can be averted only by grasping the knob and turning it as slowly as possible. Once the knob has been turned to release the latch, he can push the door open and tread silently across the plush carpeting of the bedroom to the security of the master bath.

On his way towards the bathroom door he pauses for a moment to glance down at the mass of blankets and bedspread that signifies Ilene's sleeping form. She would be very warm to curl up against, if only for a short while. The temptation to join her holds him there, staring at the pile of bedclothes that lifts with her intake of breath and then, just as unhurriedly, collapses, as if a fault line has slipped and given way. He sleeps in this bed with her less and less, it seems. The trouble is, she snores. Loudly. She is doing it now. A sonorous riffling of some pad of fleshy cartilage deep within her throat that keeps time with the heaving blankets. The nights he does sleep here he can lie awake for what seems like hours listening to this chorus of vibrating flesh, an unintentional and unlovely song meant for only him to hear. After a time, the sound will assume a new pitch or a less strident rhythm, fading away to nearly nothing, and he will drift towards sleep, but then, with a slight change of position, it will pick up again, gathering force into a huge volume of undulating sound. Amazing, he thinks, how much noise the narrow cavities within our necks and chests can produce. And what variety! Now, she is on what he thinks of as a mid-range arpeggio; interesting, in fact, now that he is standing upright and able to analyze it, that the sound goes *down* the scale in tone as she draws breath in, and stays at about the same pitch on the exhale. A low G, he would have to call it.

He watches her for another moment and envies her ignorance of this resonant song she never hears herself sing. Most mornings, she is asleep long after he leaves for the office. She has nothing in particular to wake up for, no schedule of appointments, meetings, conference calls. No email to answer, other than the ones her friends send her with mildly off-color jokes or videos of odd and amusing incidents. She has no projects on deadline or research to push forward. Sometimes he wonders how she can stand it. Her days are filled with television talk shows and leisurely late-morning chats on the phone with her lady friends and afternoons at the fitness club or the adorable shops in one of the nearby town centers, followed perhaps by a quick look at the Internet and maybe another round of late afternoon television while rustling up something for their dinner. And he envies this too: that she is totally comfortable living in this world without a job, an income, a body of work to justify her existence. It must be a kind of animal security she feels, which he has never been able to grant himself. She is here, in this life, and feels entirely justified in enjoying it. Theodore, on the other hand, has always felt a gnawing sense of inadequacy that he must repulse through the significance of his work. There has to be a purpose for his existence on this earth. If he is able to get up each day, go somewhere, and do something of use, he can feel that he has earned his place at the table, as it were. He can *be* someone.

He wants to tell her about his night, describe it to her, to see if she can discern whether it was just a dream, or something more. There must have been something more to it, something beyond this world that can merely be heard and seen and felt. But when he thinks about how he might describe what happened, he is sure he will not be able to do it justice. He will not be able to summon the words to capture and convey the gorgeous strangeness of it all. It will only sound to her like the ravings of a madman, and she does not need that now. Not after what happened in California. Not when he will have to tell her later today about the letter he has signed and will soon be submitting to Victor.

He reaches out his hand towards the heaving blanket and touches it, gently, for just a moment. His hand on her back beneath the blanket, sheets, and bedspread. Her breathing stops, interrupted by his touch, and he thinks she may wake. But then she gasps and takes a quick gulp of breath, and the blankets fall away from his fingers.

In the shower, with the door to the bathroom safely shut behind him, the water hits his back like a sheet of sound. It is a wall of heat comprised of individual notes, pellets of water that come together to make one unified mass of pressure on his skin. The sound of the shower will not wake her; it is white noise, a steady hum, not a sudden jolt or creak. He usually keeps the shower going while he shaves and dresses for precisely this reason, to cover up the other noises he might make. As he hangs his head and lets the water loosen the small, knotted muscles at the base of his neck, he thinks about how many drops of water are hitting him at this very moment. With his eyes closed, he pictures the individual jets of water that shoot from the shower head and tries to do a count: probably twenty or so around the perimeter of the head, then perhaps fifteen in the next ring in, and ten within that, and maybe five more in the middle circle. So, he could guess fifty in all. This is the work of the scientist, the way his mind has been trained to function—break things down into constituent parts, then count them, analyze them, scrutinize. Figure out how one thing leads to another, how one part fits with the next. With the basic parameters established, he can flesh out the calculation. All he needs now is a time element—drops per second, but drops is not precise enough. Molecules per second is more like it. Start with drops per second and then convert a drop to a molecule by deciding or observing how many molecules are in an average drop. Then, as he thinks about it further, the other element of the equation that must be determined is force—how fast the water is coming at him. That will determine how many drops and molecules are hitting him per second.

This is the beauty of science, what has always attracted him to it: any phenomenon or problem can be observed and analyzed and quantified this way. It's the same kind of thinking he had been trying to apply to the question of how many photons can fit in a cubic centimeter. The answer can be found, as long as the question is framed in the right way. There is definitely some similarity between the two problems. As he soaps under his armpit and leans back to rinse the shampoo from his hair, he thinks of the individual beads of water that form the stream hitting him as being analogous to individual photons, packets of light, within the waveform of light that is perceived by an observer as a consistent whole.

This is the way he wants to look at the world. Not through the lens of that wild, unruly, uncouth dream he had. That was not him, that was something totally *other*. Like having the television suddenly flip to another channel—a channel he would like to block.

Dried off and nearly dressed, he decides he will take a shave. With the shower still running to cover the noise he makes, he starts the tap in the sink, lathers his face and draws the razor across it, watching the blade scrape away the white foam, but not meeting his own eyes. He cannot bear to look there. There is nothing there he wants to see.

Thinking of his eyes makes him think about photons striking them, photons from a distant star perhaps, traversing the distance from its broiling hot surface to the cool moist surface of his retina over millions of years and trillions of miles, the same way the beads of water traveled from the surface of the shower head to the skin on the back of his neck. These things are basically the same, so why has he not been able to pin down the missing element in the question of how many photons can fit in the cubic centimeter box? There must be a missing element to the equation that he has not been able to define. He wipes the last remnants of lather from his face and dresses. He straightens his collar and slips on his shoes, another day of work ahead of him. Perhaps what has befallen him is good, this misstep that he has promoted to the level of a tragedy—perhaps it will open up more time for him to think about problems such as this. Perhaps he can let go of his ambitions and just think about things for a while, and maybe something new will come to him.

With the shower off and the light filtering through the curtains and blinds, there is a good chance he may wake her on his way out of the bedroom. That would not necessarily be a bad thing. He could tell her about his dream, or whatever it was, and put off going to the office a few minutes longer. He stops and watches the back of her head as it nods with the rhythm of her sleep. If she wakes, he could talk to her one more time as a man who has a future ahead of him, who won't be relegated to the back shelf of the structure of the Institute for the rest of his career. The back of her head always speaks to him of her innocence—she is blissfully unaware of him standing here watching her, watching her the way a parent watches a beloved child sleeping. She is unaware of what he must face at the office today; she will never be totally aware of what he must go through in the name of his profession, his job, his way of earning the money that buys them the food and clothes and gasoline for their cars. Perhaps this is what he is clinging to in this moment, watching her here. Not her, but the idea of her. Not even the idea of her, the idea of the relationship that exists between them. This is something that has been forged, built up, and twisted around them over the many years they have known each other: there is Theodore, there is Ilene, and then there is also this other, third thing that exists, which is the interaction, the relationship between them. Sometimes, in moments such as this, in which he has stopped for a second and thought of her, it raises itself up as a separate entity, and he can almost envision it as a kind of cord, a living, oblivious structure that fluctuates between them, more like a silver stream of light than a physical structure. At certain times it has grown stronger, has bound them together tighter. At other times it has loosened and seemed to unravel a bit, rays of it trailing off, turning color and dying away. Going on this trip the past weekend had brought them closer, pulled them together more in a shared adventure, the planning of it, the anticipation, holding hands together on the airplane as she read her ladies' magazine. And since the blunder at the presentation he has felt all that tightening, strengthening fall away. This separate thing that grows and fades between them has weakened, and he feels now more certain that this is what he is hanging on to as he watches the back of her head and the lump of blankets rise and fall, he is wondering what will happen to the bond between them after he endures whatever it is that will happen to him at the Institute today, whatever humiliations will come his way. Will it ever be as strong as it had been when they first arrived at the sunlit lobby of the hotel in Santa Rosa, primed for the biggest week of his professional life to unfold?

He turns from her and walks away. He grasps the doorknob and turns it—slowly—and then he is out, the door shut tight behind him. He takes the first few steps carefully, and then, as he turns the corner at the landing, hears the bed in the room behind him creak. He stops to listen. He knows this sound very well: she is up and shuffling to the bathroom. He can hear every step clearly. She is on the toilet now, he can hear the slight tinkling stream hitting the front of the bowl. He could go back to her, tell her about his vivid dream; maybe time for a kiss or something more. But he looks down at his shoes and feels it is too late. He has already primed himself for what he must do today, and this would only delay it—complicate it. Now that it is really possible to speak to her, he doesn't want to have to describe the crazy dream, he doesn't want to avoid telling her about the letter, or tell her about it and have to explain. He takes the next step and feels the world around him loosen its grip and let go of him a little more.

THE NEXT DECISION Theodore must make is easier. Driving to the commuter rail station in the next village over from his own, he sees the parking lot is unusually full for a Tuesday morning—maybe he is running late? No, the digital clock on the dash stares back at him: 7:14. A good number, seven and twice seven. But the lot *is* full, and he imagines the frustration of circling among the ranks of gleaming machines, hustling to nose his way into a spot just ahead of another harried businessman and decides to flick his left turn signal on and take the freeway instead.

Once he has merged into the flow of traffic building towards the city, he knows he has made the right choice. He can be alone with this thoughts here, without the mirror of another person's face to tell him whether he is doing something wrong.

For the most part, he stays in the right lane and goes along with the slower pace of the cars that must yield and blend with others merging from the entrance ramps every mile or so. He has tried every different method of traveling from his home to the office—commuter rail, freeway, surface streets, even carpooling with a couple of university professors from the foreign language department briefly—and has found that each route gets him to campus in roughly the same amount of time. It will take him anywhere from forty-eight to fifty-five minutes door to door. The extra effort required to shave a few minutes by hustling to catch an earlier train or weaving in and out among the more dangerous drivers in the leftmost lanes is not worth the aggravation. He allows his mind to wander, landing on whatever happens to catch his eye. A woman in the next lane over is peering into the rearview mirror and applying mascara to her lashes with her right hand as she steers with her left. A minivan coated with a thick layer of salt and winter grime has a heart traced in the dirt of the back windows with what appears to have been a girl's finger. Inside the heart is etched the somewhat startling message I LOVE MEN. The miles flow by. One freeway merges with another, and the road becomes even wider, six lanes on each side, with the commuter rail line bisecting the road down the middle, punctuated by stations at every major interchange. The traffic is light; he maintains a steady pace. The freeway emerges from the industrial wasteland of chemical tanks and warehouses that buffers his beloved suburbs from the hardscrabble wood-frame houses of the inner city. Row upon row of these drab two-story homes line the highway, perched above it on either side and giving it the feel of a tunnel. A semi-trailer changes lanes in front of him and he draws alongside it for a moment. He can feel the shuddering flanks of its trailer laden with goods, he can sense the vibrations from the pipes and mechanisms that populate the underside of the vehicle as it surges past him. There is a whimsical design on the mudflaps that bounce against the paired rear tires at the back of the truck: an image of an angry-looking semi driven by a crazed, cartoon-like man with a red handlebar mustache and a beat-up cowboy hat holding a pistol in one hand, steering wheel in the other, and the words KICKIN' ASPHALT in grubby chrome underneath.

Now the freeway makes a giant looping bend and comes back above ground level to give him his first view of the city skyline. It never fails to impress him, spread across his field of vision like a stack of multi-layered dominoes, some of them catching the first sparks of the sun as it peeks above the horizon. Another long looping turn affords him a glimpse of the gleaming lake to the east. Just a few seconds of this, and then he is back heading north, the buildings lined up again along their grid, providing the more conventional view of the city favored by the skycams for the lead-in shots to the local evening news.

He has allowed himself not to think, to let his thoughts merely flow along with the traffic. There are only a couple more miles to his exit. He glances up at his rearview mirror for some reason and catches a quick look at his own blue eye, blue surrounded by whiteness and pierced with a black hole in the middle. He sees now what has drawn his eye to the mirror: coming up behind him, a car just behind his, pressing forward, tailgating him, aggressively filling the mirror with two headlights and two bright fog lights below them and a grill that seems designed to intimidate him. In the past, having this person press him from behind like this would have nudged his blood pressure up and elicited a response from him—either speeding up to comply with the driver's insistence that Theodore go faster to accommodate him, or, more likely, slowing down to frustrate and further infuriate the tailgater. Once, when he was quite young, he tapped his brakes and nearly caused a tailgater to slam into him, provoking the enraged driver to zoom around and swerve in front of him, which forced Theodore onto the shoulder of the freeway and very nearly off the road.

Now, Theodore sees this as an opportunity to practice what he has tried to learn about staying calm. He maintains a steady speed, which just happens to be a speed that keeps the driver penned in behind him and a set of cars in the next lane that are also going about the same speed. Why does everyone want to make the world go faster? What will this man accomplish by getting around him and arriving at his office five minutes earlier than he might have? An image of time as a fluid tape measure gently undulating in a stream of warm water that flows above their heads presents itself to Theodore, the hours and minutes marked by tick marks along one side, each one passing by like the mile markers on the side of the freeway. Then, just as suddenly, the tape measure fades away, and another image draws itself to him—time expanding out from himself and the tailgating driver like a huge box above their heads, a fourth dimension they are moving through.

But this is not right.

He has envisioned time as merely the third dimension, height. He and his new friend the tailgater are traveling in a line along the first dimension, length, and it is possible that the tailgater could slam into his bumper and send him spinning out along the second dimension at an angle from the first. And the giant clear box that appeared to him is the extension of these two dimensions upwards to create the three dimensions of space. Then, he sees it: His line of sight extends to the far horizon where the road narrows down to a blurred shadow, and for a brief moment his consciousness withdraws to a point somewhere above himself, somewhere that seems to be both further within his head but also at the same moment outside and beyond it. From this new vantage point he can see the freeway in its entirety—not only the entire length of it spanning the miles from the farms beyond the city to the central core with its sky-piercing glass towers—but also the entire existence of it all at once from when the first buildings and homes and streets were torn up to make the right of way, through the bulldozers pushing earth around to dredge out the roadbed and the pouring of the first layers of gravel and cement, and then all the cars and trucks and the trains and the people milling at the stations all of them buzzing back and forth across the length of it like another layer of liquid life flowing in an ebbing and fading stream unfolding and enfolding with the cycle of every day illuminated by sunlight and then shrouded by darkness with the road lying there in its serenity beneath them, the houses torn down and replaced innumerable times, the road razed and resurfaced time and again, and then at the far end of this buzzing flow, a gradual diminishment of the flowing lights and then a complete stop where the road crumbles to dust, all of this seen as a whole: the road lying there stretched out before him like a kind of vein stripped from someone's leg with the blood of the traffic flowing over it—and the beginning and end of it and all the in between existing there at once. And it is not only that he is imagining this image of the road spread out before him, he is actually experiencing it, for just one instant, all existing there with him at one contemporaneous point. He feels it—here—now—all of it, all the millions of cars and trucks and trains and people who have passed and ever will pass over this point are here with him at this very same *Now*.

The driver behind him presses closer, flashes his brights at him. One now becomes the next.

Clearly, this man is in a hurry. He must get to the next moment in time faster than the other drivers around him. Or, what he is really trying to do, Theodore sees, is extend himself into a greater area of space than the other drivers. He cannot get to the next moment faster—all the moments come to them both at the same equivalent speed. This other man wants to take up more space in the limited span of his existence than Theodore will.

Theodore complies. The cordon of cars to their left has maintained its speed, so Theodore pushes up to seventy, moves beyond them, opens a gap for the tailgater to slither through. When the opening is just wide enough for the car to change lanes, it darts to the left and plows ahead of him. Theodore does allow himself to glance over and get a look at the tailgater passing by and sees a young woman with flattened red hair glaring at the road ahead, oblivious to Theodore and any other driver on the road, intent on her mission of getting to the next place faster than the rest.

AT THE OFFICE he avoids the secretaries and the corridor along the outside of the cubicles and makes it to his desk without encountering anybody. Slings his briefcase with the laptop in it onto the chair his visitors are supposed to use, slumps into the ergonomic chair on wheels, and punches the button that starts his desktop machine. He didn't go to the coffee shop because he didn't want to stand in the long line with the other caffeine fiends and didn't want to have to make small talk with that woman who wears two hats. This is better; alone here in his office no one will bother him.

He stares at the Degas print on the wall across from him and contemplates the dancers. One of them, the stocky, plump one whose back is reflected in the mirror, his favorite, always in the same pose, stretching her instep, pointing her toes down at the floor in a graceful drop step behind her, her other foot extended and turned at a square angle out to the right. The faint hint of a smile permanently etched on her face as she peers at the floor, lost in her work. A couple of the other dancers watch her from the side, more lithe and graceful, slimmer, they study her moves while others stretch at the bar towards the back of the room. And, what he often overlooks, seated at the bench by the piano, an old man with white hair and a full white mustache holds a violin to the crook of his neck and the bow in his other hand, about to resume playing. In the lower left corner, beneath the piano, a watering can sits, incongruously, the acute angles of the spout and handle perhaps a reference to the splayed and tortioned extension of arms and legs by these perfect human forms. He envies these young women forever captured in a moment of joy, expressing themselves through their bodies—he can almost smell the tang of female sweat and the chalk dust in the room, the late afternoon light evanescent in a dim gray winter rectangle reflected off the larger wall mirrors at the back of the room. He could stand and watch such a scene for hours, not thinking about it, not coming to any conclusions about it, just observing it and letting the sensations of the movement and sounds and smells overtake him and flow through him. He could stare at the dancers without any trace of sexual interest, merely observing the glistening forms and planes of their bodies exhibiting a kind of ever-evolving landscape that his mind could navigate, traverse. He has often looked at the stars in the night sky the same way, wondering about the distances and relationships between the pinpricks of light suspended above him, speculating about what holds them still in a seemingly-fixed firmament even as he knows they are all rushing away from each other at a speed beyond his limited comprehension. If he could stare at these things and wonder about them without having to come to any conclusions, without having to quantify them and arrange them into a paradigm, a set of mathematical rules, perhaps then he could escape the consequences of what he has done.

Pling!

The email program on his computer notifies him of a new message arriving at his inbox. Or, in this case, more than a dozen which have already been sent by the more industrious colleagues and underlings on staff. There is always a rush of morning emails flying about, Theodore feels, as a way of impressing upon others the amount of work someone is getting done—a kind of office tailgating, pushing the next guy to move a little faster.

Theodore looks at the list of boldfaced messages that have arrived in his box as yet unread. Several messages from Jerry Himmelstein, an aggressive young grad student who just came on board fall semester from Cornell. Jerry must copy him on every message he sends, no matter how trivial. A note from his friend Nick Behar in the foreign language department, one of the guys he briefly carpooled with, reminding him that they have been trying to plan a poker night with some of the other profs that never seems to fit anyone's schedule. It used to be a regular monthly event he looked forward to; now, as several months have passed without it occurring, it seems destined to slip away from them. And finally, a note marked URGENT that just arrived two minutes ago from Ji-Wan Sing, an up-and-coming Korean string theorist over by the break room. Every email from Ji-Wan is URGENT. Theodore clicks on it and opens it. Though he and Pradeep and Adams Niley are listed as recipients in the TO: line, Ji-Wan has copied nearly the entire department, including the two administrative assistants:

CC: *Steve Nulph, William Radgowski, Victor Fieldman, Amanda Nicholoff, Parag S. Punjary, A.C. Greisl, Waverly Earwood, Janice Pahud, Changyuan Nguon, Eric Christensen, Jo Anne Meranda, Rodrigo Lima, Jongsun Lin, Lloyd Neubauer, Tracy Tysdal, Douglas Hardy, Clifford Harrison, A.C. Bukta, Shin Chi Mie Atsuta, Gwo-Hwa Yuang, Jennifer Kowalczyk, Darlene Muzzarelli, Robert Onorato, Arthur D. Crookshanks, Bai Z. Kuay, Mary Kelley Cordova, Sabrina Johnson, Thomas P. Overpeck, G. Edwin Spilley, Aleksandr Veldhof, Zhongqing Zhou, Dung Pham Dong, Phyllis Raddatz, Sundaram Radhuramam*

SUBJ: *Status Update*

I received and approved your status report for the Accounting Department tracking of the Solid-State and Fluid Thermodynamics research project.

Please send to me **within one week from today** *the updated departmental file, project budget file, and any crediting documentation file. Please include with that material an updated schedule showing all key dates. You can use the attached pdf.*

No signature. No thank you. Just a note to show the rest of the world that the information Theodore provided was not quite sufficient to fill out the paperwork that Ji-Wan is responsible for compiling every month for all the ongoing federally-funded research projects at the Institute. This is the kind of message Theodore hates, but typically responds to right away with a short, polite, and supplicatory note assuring the sender that he will send the requested information as soon as possible, seeking to deflect through his own courtesy any potential build-up of animosity within the department, and thereby also showing all the people on the CC: list that he is above being harried by such a note, even though he will often carry it around with him in the back of his head the rest of the day and even into the evening if he can't pull together the information and send it right away. He has always had this need to please others, to supplicate, which has served him well enough throughout his years of navigating the academic world, even as he has risen through the ranks. Now, though, he re-reads the note and simply stares at it. It doesn't matter one whit, doesn't mean a thing to him. He doesn't immediately click REPLY or REPLY ALL as he normally might have. He pictures Ji-Wan Sing in his cubicle nervously tapping his pen, as he often does during the weekly team meetings in the conference room by the break room, and contemplates walking over to Ji-Wan and telling him that he won't be able to get this information to him any time soon—without any explanation or excuse—just to see the look on Ji-Wan's face.

Instead, he turns back to look at his dancer, at the tight black band that encircles her neck, at the reflection of the back of her neck in the mirror, her hair hanging down in a French braid; he stares at the door in the far corner of the room in the painting left open enough for a sliver of glowing golden light to shine through. His eye drifts towards the pink and yellow sheaves of sheet music on top of the piano that one of the dancers is leaning her elbow on, her other hand resting in the crook of her arm, her head craned towards the dancer in the mirror, watching her move. He has studied this painting for hours, yet he never tires of it. He always finds something new there to enchant him.

Pradeep has never understood what Theodore finds so attractive in the painting—in this painting or in any other, for that matter. On any other morning Pradeep might very well be angling his tall frame against the bookshelf on the other side of the office and telling Theodore to stop wasting his time contemplating these daubs of paint arranged in a certain way. Pradeep has freely admitted that he does not have the eye for seeing the painting the same way Theodore does, does not have the ear for hearing a piano concerto the same way—to him, as to Ilene, the painting is simply a swirl of colors, the music is merely a jumble of notes. There is no inherent beauty in one particular arrangement over another. One morning, Theodore was listening to Rachmaninov's Third piano concerto on the sound system in his office when Pradeep came by, and Theodore tried to point out to him a passage that he found exceptionally stunning, a light run up the keyboard that lingered on a trilling fifth interval at the top of the scale, and Pradeep had replied simply, "All those notes," tilting his head back in that way he has of framing his more insightful observations of scientific fact. Theodore had to laugh, for in Pradeep's musical naiveté, he had echoed one of Rachmaninov's most famously scathing critics, Aaron Copland, who once said of Rachmaninov's work, "All those notes, and to what end?"

Well, Theodore thinks, staring at the dancer's shoe, if they can't see, or hear, the beauty in it, so much the worse for them. He wouldn't want to have to live in a world as cold and empty as they do.

At any rate, the days of Pradeep stopping by his office for a chat are probably over now. He will soon be reporting to Pradeep and taking orders from him instead of from Victor, sending him status reports and expense reports and monthly updates on the progress of his next research project, most likely at this point no more than a continuation of the Plasma Dynamics grant they had been working on the past couple of years. Pradeep and he had shared a lot of happy hours together through the initial phases of scoping out that work—long afternoons at the student union with a raft of papers spread out on a table in the corner away from the bank of flat screen televisions and noisy undergrads at the video game machines, mapping out the problem of how to create the most effective gyrokinetic and gyrofluid simulations to identify ion-temperature-gradient-driven instabilities so they could get to the heart of what causes turbulence in a tokomak field device. They would trade email and text messages in the dim hours of the early morning, lobbing ideas at each other as soon as they popped into their heads, carrying on a virtual dialogue at two or three in the morning, that antipodal hour when some of their best ideas would come, the same time last night when Theodore drifted into that dream.

Now, that kind of collaboration is over. Pradeep will be busy with bigger things. He may be in Pennsylvania tending to his brother's children today, but tomorrow or the next day—whenever he returns—he will be beyond working on a project like that with Theodore again.

Theodore reaches into his briefcase and pulls out the letter. He holds it in his hand for a moment and scans it, his eye settling on the precise curves of his signature at the bottom of the page. There is nothing else he can do but deliver it to Victor. He sets it on his desk and reverts to staring at the girl held frozen in her pose, the back of her blameless head forever reflected in that mirror.

Then, in the next moment, the corner of his vision is pinched by a presence in the doorway. He swivels in his chair and motions for Victor to come in and sit.

"Teddy," Victor begins. "How are you doing today?" The question is an earnest one. Victor glances at the letter on the desk and doesn't wait for an answer. "I know this is hard on you. Hell, it's hard on me." He is talking to hear himself talk, instead of having to hear Theodore. He wants to fill up the space between them with words, a way of controlling things, limiting the damage. "I remember like it was two days ago the time a schnook by the name of Lenny Feilhaber came to me and asked me if I knew what the name of God meant. This was a kid straight out of the program at Princeton and full of himself."

Victor sits back in the chair as if he is settling in to tell a long story. "He asks me this in the hallway after a department meeting, this new kid in the department, who I barely knew. And he asks me this like he's asking for directions to the men's room." Victor scrunches his lips together into a rueful smile, his eyebrows dancing as he blinks.

"So I say to the kid, 'Don't try to be clever with me. Don't try to make yourself look good. It won't get you very far.'" Victor smiles to think of it, the impression his words must have made on the young man. Theodore has seen similar situations unfold in staff meetings and in the corridors of the building here over the years, where a stray word or glance from Victor could ruin a young scientist's day or week. "The kid never spoke to me again. I think I spooked him. He only stayed here six months into a two-year fellowship, it must have been." Victor looks over at Theodore and at the letter folded on the desk between them like a sliver of stray sunlight that has broken loose from the painting on the wall behind him. "But I'll tell you what. That kid put his head down and worked the entire time he was here. He did his job. And he went on to Caltech and became a fine physicist. I met him again a few years ago at a conference in Vienna and listened to him present some very nice work on strong particle interactions."

Theodore knows now why Victor has been telling him this story, and recognizes Feilhaber's name because it has now been attached to a piece of research he remembers. But he remains silent, out of fear and out of respect for the situation he has placed himself in, and lets Victor finish his story.

"The kid settled down and did his work. And he put himself in position to be involved with a couple of other gentlemen you may have heard of who together, the three of them, won the Nobel Prize a couple of years ago."

"I remember."

"Yes, they won the Prize for their work on asymptotic freedom in strong interaction." Victor smiles at Theodore and rubs his forehead, knowing he has made his point. "So, you see, my friend, there is something to be said for going off in a corner somewhere and putting your head down and doing some work that may not appear to be very sexy or on the leading edge for a while. Something very valuable may be hiding there, and this could be an opportunity for you, to not have to worry so much about what it takes to get ahead and bother with all the crap that goes on with running the department." He scratches a raw patch of skin on his wrist where his watch seems to be too tight.

Victor is about to say something more, but he's interrupted by the jingling beeps of his cell phone erupting in his pants pocket. With some effort, Victor lifts his hips up out of the chair so that he can fish the beeping phone out of his pants and answer it before the call goes away.

"Yes. He's sitting right here." A brief pause, during which Victor's eyes search Theodore's face as if he expects to find a hidden meaning there. "I'm in his office."

Theodore returns Victor's look, trying to decipher who the caller may be, and why they are asking about him. The look on Victor's face has turned from one of questioning to one of distraction. He has turned his eyes away from Theodore and is staring into space now, the center of his brow contorted into a deep crease of concern.

"Yes, I'll call you back."

Victor clicks the phone call away, and looks over at Theodore, his cheeks flushed with what may be anger or may be panic.

"What's the meaning of this . . . this email?" He reaches the phone over to Theodore and shows him an open message on the device. Theodore takes the phone and starts reading, skimming through the tiny lines of text. None of this is registering with him. Something very bad must have happened for Victor to be reacting this way, and then he reads further and a glimmer of recognition takes shape in his mind. Some of the words he sees in the message appear to be words he has himself written a few hours ago, in the middle of the night. *"There is a unity to everything, from the largest forms to the smallest. The spiral spinning of a galaxy is the same form embodied in the twist of light that comprises the most minuscule particles of matter."* And further down, as he thumbs through the message by brushing his fingertip against the phone: *"Light is conscious energy, the medium of thought, and thought is all there is, a giant timeless thought."*

He hands the phone back to Victor and looks at him with an empty pit of dread in his stomach. As he hands the phone to him, he glances at the address and the subject line at the top of the note and sees that it is indeed the note he jotted down in the middle of the night and sent to himself. But how, he wonders, how could it have gone to Victor and to whomever it was that phoned to tell him about it? He looks at Victor and is at a loss for what to say. Perhaps it is only a minor problem. He can explain to him exactly what happened, that he was just sending himself some notes, some ramblings from the middle of the night, half-baked ideas that don't amount to anything, and leave it at that. Then give Victor the letter to sign and be done with the whole thing.

"What were you thinking?" Victor's face is bright red as he says this. His voice is a low, barely-controlled growl.

"I wasn't thinking. These are just some notes I was jotting down, some ideas that came to me in the middle of the night." But there must be something more to this, a reason Victor is so furious about it.

Theodore swivels his chair to see the inbox on his desktop machine. He sees the note he sent to himself near the bottom of the list, dated 2/16/--, 3:27 a.m. There is no subject on the note, and no other recipients but himself. Then he thinks to click the Sent Items folder and sees something strange—the same note, with no subject, sent by himself to dozens of other people at 9:47 a.m., just a few moments ago.

Victor's phone chimes again. He answers it before the second set of tones. "Yes . . . he's still here. No, I didn't sign it." Victor will not look at him, he's staring at the window behind him instead. "No—of course not." He hasn't seen Victor sweat this much in all their many years of working together. During a long pause in which Victor is listening to whomever is on the other end of the call, Theodore feels the hole in the pit of his stomach grow. He knows something terrible has happened, and looks again at the list of names in the TO: line of the message on his screen. There, somehow, is a list of recipients that appears to include most, if not all, of the physicists who attended his presentation in California, as well as most, if not all, of the research fellows here at the Institute—dozens of people received this message, dozens of his most esteemed colleagues in String Theory and particle physics.

"Of course," Victor says, glancing over at Theodore, his eyes barely able to stay fixed on Theodore's face. "Right away."

Theodore looks straight ahead, not wanting to meet Victor's eyes, waiting for the other shoe to drop, hoping for this moment to disappear.

"Teddy, that was the Chairman of the Board of Directors, in town for the board meeting tomorrow. This email, this message from you, means I have to let you go. I have to fire you. They say this is grounds for terminating your employment, and I have to agree. This message . . ." He stares at the words on his phone again and blinks his eyes, as if he can't believe what he is seeing. "The future of this Institute, our funding and our reputation are at stake." The words are like splinters of metal cutting through Theodore's face. "What the hell were you thinking?"

Theodore doesn't know what to say. He hadn't intended the message to go to anyone but himself. And he's not sure how it could have been sent to anyone else. At the moment the message was apparently broadcast to the entire String Theory community, he had been staring wistfully at the back of that dancer's neck in the print on the wall of his office—hell, he hadn't even thought about the note since he sent it last night.

Something isn't right here; something doesn't add up. That's all Theodore can think, as he tries to frame a response to Victor's question. But then, nothing has seemed to go the way he thought it would since the moment he discovered he lost his notes in the lobby of that hotel. He never envisioned that his life could spin this wildly out of control within a few days, over a few misplaced and misconstrued words. He still wants to work here, at the Institute, in whatever capacity they will have him. That's what Victor's story was driving at a few moments ago—he was prepared to simply let him go off in a corner by himself, collect his comfortable salary and daydream about whatever it is he wants to think about. And now this—whatever this is. He still cannot believe that Victor has said he is going to fire him, that he could turn against him so quickly, over such a trivial matter.

"I don't know what to say." Theodore looks at Victor, tries to make eye contact with him, to rebuild with his eyes the relationship that his words have destroyed, to restore the connection between them. But Victor will not meet him; he's looking instead at the letter on the desk. "I'll sign the letter," Theodore says, watching Victor's eyes. "I already did sign it. I'll do anything you say—I know I was wrong."

Victor won't look at him; he has already moved on. Whatever friendship had been there between them doesn't matter anymore.

"I'm sorry. Some things are bigger than any one person." Yes, Theodore knows, he has seen something much bigger than this Institute only a few hours ago, in the monstrous vision that is quietly fading into the recesses of his memory. Victor stands and is ready to leave—he wants this to be over with now, as soon as it can possibly be.

Theodore watches him stand to go and wants to latch on to him, to hold him with some other plea for a reasonable solution to this—he still cannot believe that a simple email message, a harmless message he sent to himself, could mean the end of his career as a scientist. What could really be so terrible in that note that would warrant an outcome such as this? Yes, he did mention consciousness again—*thought, a giant thought.* Yes, he said that again, and perhaps on top of what happened at the conference the other day this is the capper, the final straw. But he didn't say anything about God, didn't use the word, that he can recall. What has he done that is so very wrong?

Theodore wants to scan the note one more time, to see if he can make a case for himself. "Wait." There has to be something he can say in his own defense.

He pulls the note up on his own phone and skims through it—it isn't really very long. A few paragraphs, a couple hundred words . . . *the spiral is a two-dimensional slice of the three dimensional form of all matter . . . The shape of a tree, and an apple, and a cyclone emulate this outward flowing . . . every particle, quark and lepton and gluon that conspires to generate these forms is created by light . . . To us the universe is expanding at an ever-accelerating rate because we cannot measure eternity or infinity.*

What is wrong with these statements? They seem now, as he reads them, in the pallid light of a February morning, to be merely weak attempts to grasp at some glimmers of meaning that may have seeped through a restless night of sleep. But then he nudges the screen of his phone a bit faster and scrolls all the way to the end. There, at the bottom of the page, the last thing he jotted down, an afterthought really, an equation that would make any scientist reel:

$0 \times \infty = 1$

Zero times infinity equals one.

Absurd.

Of course, now he sees it. On top of all the other things that have happened since Friday, these five symbols arranged this particular way are enough to spell out his doom. No scientist in his right mind would write such an equation and send it out to his most esteemed colleagues. Not even a scientist who told them in a big hotel ballroom that they ought to consider God as part of the equation. It simply doesn't make any sense—'doesn't add up,' as Victor is fond of saying.

He looks over at his friend of twenty years and knows that he is through.

How did this get copied to everyone? That's his final thought—how did it happen? But it does not matter. It is done, it is out there. He looks at the letter he signed, still lying there crisp and clean on the desk as if it were still of some use, then he puts on his coat, picks up his briefcase without even unplugging his laptop and putting it in, and walks past Victor without saying another word.

THERE ARE MOMENTS when nothing around him seems real, when he feels as if he is moving through a dream. This is one of them. With his briefcase slung over his shoulder, he trudges down the outer corridor with the window offices of the research fellows on his right, the cube maze on his left. He is just moving, floating. Going forward, one step after another. He doesn't see anyone in the offices he marches past, and he doesn't care whether they see him. He is gone, he is no longer a part of this, and they will carry on without him. He is no longer a part of any of this, the research, the staff meetings, the committee meetings, the all-expense-paid conferences in far-off countries, the workaday feeling of just grinding through, pushing through until something good and useful comes of a day. Those things are gone.

The office is nearly silent. The whispering outflow of dehydrated air pumping through the ventilation system is the only sound, punctuated by someone up ahead pecking away at the keyboard of their computer. The tapping of the keys grows louder as he approaches—one of the associates chatting on a forum or plowing through some email. Yes, it's Ji-Wan, he sees the back of his head now, coarse, lank black hair thinning to a bald spot at the top his skull, collared light blue dress shirt with short sleeves, oddly enough. This registers—one of Ji-Wan's quirks: he wears short-sleeved shirts in all seasons, even through the bitter cold of the Midwestern winters. Ji-Wan, generating more of his tone-deaf and slightly strident email messages for the department to read. Well . . . good for him. He will be here sitting in his cubicle, typing away the rest of today, and tomorrow, and the next day. And what will Theodore be doing— smarter than all the rest—what will Theodore be doing the rest of today, and tomorrow, and the day after that?

As he shoves the door open that leads him out of the huddled warmth of the building and into the quad, the air that strikes him feels like a wall, so great is the contrast between the artificial warmth of the interior and the great mass of cold he is stepping into, as if he is stepping out of an airplane into the middle of the sky.

The quad is bustling at this hour, students running late for the last round of morning classes, backpacks slung across their shoulders, boys and girls alike—young people with their entire futures ahead of them, single-minded in their pursuit of the next pleasure, the next adventure.

At first he starts to head across the wide expanse of the north quad towards the faculty lot where he always parks his car. This is the automatic path he would take when leaving the building, heading home. But there is nothing to go home to; he cannot imagine facing Ilene with this news at this hour, arriving home before lunch, startling her in the middle of her daily routine. Perhaps he could call and warn her first, but the thought of breaking this news to her on the phone doesn't seem right. It will have to be in person, and it will have to wait. He has no blueprint for how to handle a situation such as this. He only knows that he cannot go home yet.

He follows a girl walking alone towards one of the liberal arts buildings, political science, economics, languages, where some of his friends from the faltering poker group teach. She is compact, petite, her bottom maybe half the size of Ilene's, her blond hair shaped into a thick wedge at the back, not concealed by a cap. Like the others on campus, she is weighed down by a grungy gray and green backpack, overloaded with textbooks.

She reminds him of a girl he dated briefly in his own undergrad years, a tiny political science major, full of life—his intellectual equal, who could outmaneuver him in any debate that concerned the slippery concepts surrounding the systems human beings have designed to control one another. He has always preferred the solid world of physical facts, phenomena that can be calculated and observed. Everything she had told him about the courses in her major seemed to involve an artificial world that man dreamed up—and then he found once he got into grad school that these kinds of *de facto* political systems existed everywhere and had to be navigated carefully. He had always been good at being careful, being correct.

The girl veers from the tarmac path and charges up the steps that lead to the lecture hall, a grand faux-gothic cathedral of learning, a mixture of limestone and touches of brick with withered strands of ivy clinging to the walls. Sometimes he thinks it is these buildings and their look of a medieval sanctuary of wisdom that counts for more than the faculty inside as a means of recruiting new students and maintaining the reputation of the university. When he looks at the overhead panorama of the campus proudly displayed on the brochures and web sites to lure the students and their parents in, he can't help but think of how much money flows through this place in the form of grants and endowments: the millions parents pay in tuition is hardly even necessary to keep the place going. The quad speaks not only of learning, but also of wealth—the wealth that only knowledge and a degree can bring. The students who go here now realize that they are here not only to learn, but to earn They are not as idealistic as he had once been. Perhaps they have simply grown up faster, but they seem to behave like young initiates to a select form of country club.

As the girl disappears within the building, he finds he cannot resent her though. He only feels a deep sense of detachment, as if he is looking at her through a second pair of eyes set deeper within his head. Withdrawn from the ones he has been accustomed to using.

There is a hiking trail, an urban bike path that leads away from the campus just beyond the liberal arts building—Lyman Hall. Every building on campus here is not just a building, it is a Hall. Even his own former office in the modernistic science building was actually housed in Foster Hall, which he always thought sounded more like a men's clothing retailer. To avoid sounding pompous, he had preferred using the basic street address for the building on his business cards and email signature: Room 157, 6054 South Woodlawn Avenue.

The trail leads west, away from the lake and away from campus. In the days ten years ago when they first converted this former rail line into a bike path, students rarely ventured more than a few hundred yards from campus for fear of being raped or mugged. There was talk of closing the trail—the few pioneers who were not afraid to use it were putting themselves in danger, and the residents of the neighborhood whose houses backed onto it feared it would provide an easy access point for burglars and drug pushers. Now Theodore doesn't think twice about wandering away from campus along the path. The neighborhood has been revitalized by the influx of students, and there is a plan to extend the trail even further west, into the heart of the most dangerous neighborhoods in the city, as a catalyst for re-development.

This is good, he thinks, walking this way, away from campus, away from everything he is leaving behind. After a few hundred yards, the last remnants of the campus are behind him, the path is lined on either side by the back gardens of slightly rundown woodframe houses—former family homes now subleased as rentals for grad students and upperclassmen. Homes for the lower tier of associate profs, clerks, and admins to lease. Twenty years ago this was a ghetto. Now the yards have been cleaned up and there are gates in the fences and garden walls to allow for access to the trail.

The path is nearly deserted at this hour, classes in session, midday Tuesday. Only a stray biker or jogger disrupts the tunnel of his vision looking down the trail. After a few blocks, the houses are replaced by a loose constellation of businesses, lining a minor thoroughfare. The backside of a liquor store littered with stacks of broken cardboard boxes, a vending machine that does not display the friendly red and white swirl of a Coke can, but instead is dressed all in black with a pair of scowling green snake eyes and a menacing slogan: PIERCING ENERGY THAT STRIKES BACK.

He has to stop and look both ways before crossing the street—motorists are not expected to yield to pedestrians here, the car is king. On the other side of the avenue, he sees the grungy backside of another retail block, with signs that cater to passersby on the trail: ELGIN WATERCARE, BISCUITS CAFÉ and CLASSIC CLEANERS – TAN & LAUNDRY.

Maybe he should stop at one of these places. He hesitates—maybe the café; he hasn't had any coffee yet today and his head is pounding from the lack of caffeine. But the open trail ahead of him seems more appealing. He doesn't want to have to speak to anyone just yet. As he walks on into the residential neighborhood again, he feels an odd sense of elation. When was the last time he took a walk in the middle of a week day, by himself, with nothing else to occupy his mind? It is as if he has been walking through a flat desert plain and suddenly stepped to the precipice of the Grand Canyon, a huge hole spread out before him with nowhere to go but out and *down*. As one foot steps ahead of the other, he wonders what he will do next. But there is no next. There is only the quiet scuffling of his footsteps and the faint brush of the wind against the bare damp branches of the trees. He has been released from the tube of daily commitments that has shaped his thoughts for years, the cyclical churning of the same half dozen items on his mental to do list for his various projects, tumbling through his brain like laundry in a dryer. For the first time in a very long time, no one on earth knows where he is or what he is doing.

Ahead, on his right, is a small widening of the path where a couple of red metal benches have been placed—a rest stop. And, also, he sees as he approaches, there is a mile marker set in blue and green tile in the center of the semi-circle defined by the benches. This is mile 5.0. And beyond the two benches, just off the trail, is a curious thing—a bronze sundial planted in the middle of a low stone column. He approaches it and sees the faint shadow cast by the sharp edge of the bronze blade. According to the dial, it is just past 11:30, which seems about right.

He doesn't want to look at his phone to verify it, the phone with its email messages and text messages and downloadable pop tunes, which has also obviated the need for wearing a watch. The flat top of the column has etched lines fanning away from the tip of the blade, pointing to the hours carved in roman numerals into the stone. And at the bottom of the face of this "clock" is a motto also etched in stone: THE HEAVENS DECLARE THE GLORY OF GOD.

He looks up, off to his right, through the willowy branches of the trees. The sun is a faint yellow ball, low to the horizon even at mid day, so weak through the scattering haze that he can stare at it for a couple of seconds without having to look away. What was that calculation he had been thinking about, earlier this morning? How many photons are striking him, or the blade of this sundial, each second? The question seems absurd now, beyond his ability to comprehend. How could he have ever thought he could answer a question such as this?

Instead of thinking about it, he gazes up at the sun again and closes his eyes, allowing the tranquil light to varnish a nebulous orange patch on the underside of his eyelids. As he stands there, his face held up to the sky, a thought slips across his awareness: he opens his eyes and thinks: I am staring directly at the center of the solar system. This doesn't seem like much of a revelation, but the more he thinks about it, the more fantastic it seems. Rather than a person, a man, standing rooted to the ground, he begins to feel himself as a patch of awareness, looking out across the millions of miles towards the huge ball of nuclear fire, towards the star, that is at the center of a system of planets. And in doing so, he starts to get a feel for the relative position of the earth and his place on it—his head pointing away from the planet and towards the center of the solar system, the planet even as he does so spinning him at thousands of miles an hour to the left and away from the center. This feeling of looking at the center of the solar system makes him think of all the movements he is undergoing even as he is standing here perfectly still—the earth rotating him away from the sun, the earth revolving him around the sun, the sun and all its planets and belts of icy rock coursing through the Local Interstellar Cloud and the Local Bubble, remnants of a relatively recent supernova, only a few hundred million years old. Through the Orion arm of the galaxy and around the center of the galaxy, which would be above him, beyond him, if he were to look up here again later tonight. He can feel the earth and the sun spinning through space, spiraling around each other in a giant helix as they hurtle along in their relative paths, all these movements spinning, spinning him up and out of himself until there is nothing left but himself, his eyes closed again for a moment, his mind empty and numb, nothing left but this tiny patch of awareness at the center of all these spiraling motions.

When he opens his eyes again there is a moment, a brief instant, in which he can see in every direction at once. He sees the trees and the path in front of him and also the path behind him, the shops at the intersection in the distance, the houses and their ramshackle gardens and back yards to either side. He can see his shoes and the cuffs of his pants and the composition of the pavement beneath them and above him the milky pale overcast of the sky. It is as if he has opened up, as if somebody lifted a tarp away from his eyeballs, uncovering his brain, and he can finally see beyond it, clearly, everything there is to see.

His eyelids shudder and blink, then blink again, and the vision is gone.

THE DOORWAY TO the bar is inset from the sidewalk and sheltered from the cold. Theodore stands there for a moment and stares at what the wind has rustled into this compressed space surrounded by brick walls: dead leaves, crisp and rotten, their colors leached away by months of being blown and tossed across the city streets, a candy wrapper and a used rubber glove, its shrunken see-through simulation of a human hand looking more like the withered white carcass of a jellyfish that has washed up on the shore.

Perhaps he is just hungry—perhaps that is what made him grow lightheaded a few moments ago. Hungry and cold. He can warm up in here and have a sandwich, something to drink. He has not eaten anything since dinner at the restaurant yesterday evening, before the symphony.

A bell attached to the top of the door announces his entrance; his eyes take a moment to adjust to the light. There are only a couple of people seated at the bar and a handful of empty tables lined up against the wall of windows along the side of the building that faces the street. He would rather sit at one of the tables by himself, but the man seated at the counter looks at him as if he might be offended if he did not join him. Theodore slings his briefcase onto one of the high wooden chairs, shrugs off his coat, and hoists himself into another chair, not directly next to the man, but close enough to not appear unfriendly. At the far end of the bar, near the door to the kitchen, a young woman sits smoking a cigarette and gazing at the television perched high above for all to see. The bar has adopted a north woods theme for its decoration, camping and hunting gear adorning the knotty pine wall behind the counter, fishing rods, the head of what appears to have been a real twelve-point buck mounted at the far end of the room, though the wilderness atmosphere is marred by several neon signs advertising national brands of beer and a large poster of the schedule from the past season of the local professional football team, including sweating bottles of beer adorned with the helmets of the team instead of bottle caps, lined up in a formation that simulates a winning touchdown pass.

It takes a while for the young woman to abandon her cigarette and attend to Theodore, as if his appearance here is an unwanted distraction from more important business she is tracking on the television. When she does come over, she approaches him not from behind the bar, but between him and the other patron, standing to his left and perching her elbows on the empty chair between them, as if her body is an unbearable weight she must prop up.

"Hey," she says, uncertainly. Perhaps she is not a waitress? For a moment, Theodore is left to wonder. He nods, to acknowledge her presence. Then she adds, as an afterthought: "Can I get you something?"

"Yeah, she'll get you something. She'll get you whatever you want." The burly man to the left of them laughs at his small joke, chuckling mostly to himself, but loud enough to let them know he was angling for a laugh. Then he returns to the task of shoveling a forkful of food to his mouth, bobbing his head as he chews, to confirm the validity of his statement. "Whatever you want," he repeats through a mouthful of chewing.

"Put a lid on it, Wayne." The waitress says this in a weary way that conveys how many times she has heard such things from him before. Throughout all this, Theodore has had a chance to browse the menu, but doesn't see anything that looks particularly appetizing.

"Do you have coffee?"

"We can do that. There's probably some left." Left from when? "You want anything to eat?"

He does want something, but nothing from here.

"I'm fine for now, thank you."

When Theodore finds himself in uncomfortable situations, he tends to become even more formal than usual, a safeguard, a way of putting distance between himself and those around him.

The waitress slinks back towards the kitchen and disappears in search of his coffee. In her absence, his sudden companion has seized the opportunity to start lecturing, the man's face lit by the blue incandescence of the screen looming above them, his voice urged into an aggressive tone by the tiny jabbering voices falling on them from the ceiling.

"See, they'll take any chance they can to promise something for nothing." The man inhales and tilts his head at the screen to indicate who he is talking about. "You think health care is expensive now, just wait until it's free. That's what they want you to believe, that's what they're selling—something for nothing. As if you could pull a bunch of doctors and drugs and hospital rooms out of a hat. These bastards will do anything to take money out of your pocket and mine, and give it to people who haven't worked a day in their lives."

The mention of these others, whoever they may be, has served to infuriate the man. Theodore watches him as his face assumes a deeper shade of pink, his eyes squinting as he veers his attention from the debating pundits on the screen towards Theodore. The man's hands drop the knife and fork onto the plate and leap in Theodore's direction. "See, you and me, we work for a living. We pay for our health care, out of our own pockets. And these bastards want to take your money and pay for some deadbeat's birth control pills and abortions and prescription pain killers and I say let's ship them all back to Mexico where they came from. Let 'em figure out how to have a health care plan of their own down there."

Wayne is his name, Theodore remembers that now—the waitress called him Wayne. Wayne's face has become more plastic, his jowls loosened and expanded by the words coming out. Near the temples, directly above, Theodore can see a branching network of broken capillaries outlined in purple and blue against the soft pink skin of his face, fanning out from a single spot where a tiny vein approaches the surface of the skin. Theodore nods in agreement, uncertain about exactly what the man's point is, but not wanting to contradict him in his agitated state.

"So," Wayne says, "you look like you rake in a good paycheck, highly qualified. Whaddeya work at a bank or something? You're exactly the kind of guy, you and me, who these bozos in Congress are trying to rip off."

Theodore doesn't want to tell him what he used to do, or what just happened to him only an hour or two ago. It still does not seem real enough to relate to another person. Perhaps there will be a phone call from Victor telling him to come back to the office, it was all a mistake. He imagines them all there sitting in their cubes and at their desks, pecking away at their computers, talking in the conference room and the break room over bowls of microwave chili and vending machine snacks. This is about the time of day when the pressures of the first two waves of morning email wind down, and some serious thinking time, that long stretch between about one-thirty and four, can begin; he always thought of the afternoon as a kind of nap time, a siesta for the brain, where lazy staff meetings would drag on and an occasional free spell would engender some real creative talk about ways to attack the entangled equations scribbled across a white board. But the good paycheck Wayne has associated with him is gone. There may never again be another paycheck as good as what was automatically deposited in his bank account last week. That's what is most disconcerting about this train of thought—the idea of having to wonder about where the money will come from. He hasn't had to worry about money since his post-doc fellowship days. The money has always just showed up in his accounts, like magic. Even so, the money was never his primary concern. He did the work, sent the emails, filled out the reports—but deep down, he was always working towards the idea that he might someday stumble upon the one big thing, the final answer, the Theory of Everything.

He would sometimes picture it in his head, on his way to work, or leaning back and looking out his window at the quad—not what the Theory of Everything would look like itself necessarily, but what it would feel like to have discovered it. He would assume the feeling of being The One, the next Einstein, the next Newton. The One who got it all right. He can picture it even now, as he lifts his head towards the blue light of the television and closes his eyes, a kind of deep stillness and peace settling over him—the peace of total satisfaction and knowing. Yes, there would be two different and highly pleasurable sensations: the joy of having achieved what so many others have strived for over the years, the attainment of what had eluded so many gifted minds, and then also, beyond the accolades of colleagues and the acknowledgment of genius by the wide world beyond, there would be the even greater satisfaction of really knowing, perhaps as no one else could know, exactly how it all works—every last piece of it, from the largest scale structures of space and time down to the most insignificant clockwork of the tiniest elementary particles. With the discovery of that one final principle, that one unifying theme—yes, that is how he pictures it, more a *theme* than an equation, but certainly it would be something that could be reduced or expressed as an equation—with that one theme, he could look at anything, any one aspect of the universe and say to himself or any other—even a man as bedeviled by the workaday world as Wayne here on his left—he could say to them, yes, of course, this is how it works. We understand it all now, thanks to me.

"They'll sort it all out."

Theodore surprises himself as much as he does Wayne, when these words come out of his mouth. He's not even sure why he has said it. Perhaps just to shut Wayne up, or see what he will say next.

"Yeah, you say that, and it's guys like you who really do have something to lose and don't have the guts to stand up to them who will get burned in the end."

The waitress is back now with Theodore's cup of coffee. She sets it before him on the counter with special care, as if she brewed it specifically for him. Perhaps she did. She can sense that the conversation has heated up, so she retreats to her corner of the bar and her dying cigarette without a word.

"Something out of nothing, that's what they all want. Hell, you could just as soon turn one of those coals into a loaf of bread as do what they say they will do."

Wayne nods in the direction of an open brazier on the floor behind the bar, in which a pile of charcoal is smoldering beneath a wire rack. This is probably in keeping with the wilderness theme—it may even be a way of helping to heat this place. Wayne's assertions have brought Theodore down from whatever high orbit he had attained when he felt he was viewing the motions of the sun and the earth in their flight across the heavens, from whatever transfiguration had caused him to spin into the realm of those whirling and wistful ramblings about infinity he sent in that e-mail message meant only for himself. His only concern now is how to tell Ilene about what he has done, how to frame his latest and most fatal blunder in a way that will ease the shock to her. But there is no way around it—he no longer has a job, no longer has a steady paycheck to pay for things like health insurance and their mortgage and their monthly night out on the town. They will have to sell the house and move to something smaller, an apartment maybe. Perhaps Ilene will have to find some line of work herself, her afternoons talking on the phone with friends, lounging in front of the flat screen TV a thing of the past. The future he sees spread out before them is one of dwindling opportunities, diminishing pleasure, struggle and hardship. How will she react to the news? There is no way to know until the words come out of his mouth—perhaps she will leave him. Perhaps that living visceral cord that has joined them together over the years will finally fray and fall apart under the strain.

Wayne is correct about one thing; in his heart of hearts Theodore has known this all along: There is no other reality than what he can see before him with his own two eyes. There is no way to transmute those burning coals into something entirely other, except by the means prescribed by the laws of physics. If he were to stay here the rest of the afternoon—and what else does he have to do?—Theodore could watch as the coals slowly burn themselves out, converting each molecule of the impure carbon briquettes by combustion into heat, light, and reaction products released as the trace odor of smoke that permeates the room. And that faint star above him too will burn itself out in somewhat the same manner, an immense downward spiral of combustion, just as surely as the other stars in the universe will, over time, cool down and drift apart and disintegrate until there is nothing left but a vast and empty nothingness, an absence of all heat and all light and all coherent particles of matter, nothing but the absolute zero null and void from whence Theodore and Wayne and Ilene and all the rest of this came.

4

THIS CHURCH IS falling apart. He can see that clearly enough. To Theodore's great surprise, the blue door at one side of the giant limestone building yielded to his tug on the handle and opened right up, granting him access to the warmth of the building. Anyone could simply walk in, just as he did, and wander around the building, just as he is now, looking for things to steal if they so chose, or, as Theodore is now, merely looking for another place to get in out of the cold, dark February afternoon. This old place is a warren of cramped passageways and empty rooms used for what? The building must be at least a hundred years old, and he can see signs of its general deterioration, its slow and inevitably losing battle against entropy.

Disarray is everywhere. He pokes his head inside one of the many rooms that line this corridor and sees what might on occasion be used as a Sunday school classroom, but might also be nothing more than a storage room for miscellaneous church-related junk. There is a pile of musty hymnals strewn haphazardly on top of a radiator and windowsill; a loose assortment of metal folding chairs arranged in no particular manner in the same far corner of the room; a bulletin board with a sheet of ruled notebook paper pinned to it containing a list of children's names and a few check marks next to them as well as a few dull golden stars for attendance or assignments completed that are curling and about to fall at any moment to the floor. On the wall at the opposite end of the room, someone—a child, a teacher—once stapled the first few letters of a Bible verse cut meticulously with scissors out of fading yellow construction paper: NOW THESE ARE; there is a pile of towels and bathrobes and motheaten men's dress shirts and neckties; there is an old upright piano probably used to play along with hymns the children might have sung. He steps to it and runs his right hand up the C scale. The tension in the keys has come unsprung; the strings are loose and out of tune. The pale green paint on the wall above the radiator is peeling; chips of it litter the pile of leather-bound hymnals, their pages thin and brittle and just as prone to crumbling into dust as the leaves that littered the doorway of the tavern he left several hours ago. Everything has a tendency to disorder; everything is falling apart. It takes energy, work, applied to any system, any *thing*, such as the objects in this room, to keep them in good order, to keep them from disintegrating into a loose and random collection of atoms. There must be a constant application of energy to every thing, every person, to keep it from returning back to randomness and cold.

He goes back to the corridor and follows it to another larger room that looks as if it might be a kind of library. How long had he been outside after leaving Wayne and his depressing talk of government health insurance—two or three hours perhaps? He had wandered aimlessly around the neighborhood, looking at storefront windows filled with nothing he wanted, staring at anyone who had happened to pass by with the certain understanding that they could provide no manner of assistance with the problem he has yet to solve. What he has found interesting in the course of this day is how time and space have *opened up*, the extent to which his concept of his self has until now defined his relationship to everything he perceived. He saw a giant acacia tree guarding a tiny bungalow and stood there on the buckling sidewalk observing its roots and the leathery bark of the tree, watching it, staring at it for several minutes, as if it might yield some secret to him about its existence. In standing there, examining the tree, without his own idea of who *he* was—scientist, physicist—or where he needed to be, or what he should be doing, he began to feel a sense of relationship to the tree, both of them living creatures, both of them complex mechanisms for converting energy into form, coherent structure, both of them extravagant localized systems of order fighting against the downward gradient of entropy, the tendency for things to fall apart. He could feel the tree standing there before him, dormant, waiting, waiting for the first few gusts of warm air and glimpses of the sun to suck in and trigger itself back to life. He went up to the tree and touched one of its many hooked thorns, each of them an inch or two long, protruding from the branches of the tree at random intervals. He held the ball of his thumb against the pointy tip of the thorn and, in that brief moment, felt as if he could sense the tree poised there, even in its dormant state, feeling the slight and elusive pressure of him as an intruder.

Later, he had watched a dog amble across the street, a collie mix it had appeared, ears pinned back against its head, eyes squinting into the wind. Where was the dog going? What thoughts moved across its brain, telling it where to go, what to do? He felt just as aimless and unsure as the dog must be—no, moreso. The dog must have had more of a sense of itself than he did at that moment, some purpose it was pursuing, perhaps headed back to its master's home, perhaps in the direction of a garbage heap where it knew some particularly choice scraps might be found. His only motivation is one of avoidance, avoiding being himself, this new self that is no self, that has nothing familiar or acceptable to hold on to.

In the library room, books are strewn along one low shelf in no discernable order. There is a series of Christian self-help titles and a set of travel magazines that feature destinations in the Holy Land called *Footsteps in Faith*. In one corner of the room, a stack of beat up children's board games, "Monopoly," "Risk," "Candy Land," and another one called "The Bridges of Shangri-La." Time has come to a standstill—he feels as if he could stand here staring at these things and listening to himself breathe for a very long time without moving or without wanting to move. He could stay here and just watch whoever might enter the room without any interaction with them whatsoever. What need is there to interact? Perhaps there is a place where they will let him do this—just exist, taking in sensations of sound and color and motion, without any need to process them into data, without any reason for doing anything with these bits of information. All his life he has been directed towards a purpose, towards a goal. Now that he has nothing to move towards, the most natural thing to do appears to be just standing still and letting whatever comes along pass over him.

In one corner of the room he has come to think of as the library, though it hardly qualifies as such, he finds a small refrigerator, no taller than his waist, the kind undergrad students keep in their dorm rooms for leftover slices of pizza and bottles of beer. He opens the fridge and sees it is empty save for a plastic jug of apple juice and a torn package of shortbread cookies, snacks for a Sunday school class. Suddenly, his appetite rears up—he is ravenous—he has not eaten anything since the restaurant meal he shared with Ilene before the symphony the night before; ages ago it seems. He pops the plastic lid off the jug and lifts it to his mouth, letting the cool, slippery liquid slide down his throat. He can barely even taste it, but as he takes a second gulp, he realizes that the juice is not quite right—the granules of apple flavoring have separated and settled to the bottom of the jug. He checks the rim of the jug's mouth and sees that the juice is several months past the sell-by date. No matter—it still tasted good, still feels good as it nestles into his stomach. He grabs the package of cookies and pops one of them whole into his mouth. Chewing, he realizes these are very old too. The cookie is virtually tasteless, bland, soft and crumbly, but he savors it as he chews and swallows—anything tastes good after not having eaten for nearly a day. He takes another cookie from the package and bites into it. He does not need much more than this—a warm place to stay, a few bites of food to sustain him. All the rest is over-elaboration.

As he finishes the last bit of shortbread, he hears a sound, a low-pitched rumbling that lifts and builds to a high crescendo. At first it is hard to make out, then it registers—it is coming from the corridor to his right. He leaves the library and heads towards it; another turn down a hallway towards the center of the building, the walls lined with old-fashioned paintings of former deacons and ministers of the church from the past hundred and fifty years, all of them dead and gone.

Here, the sound of voices lifted up. He goes through a set of double doors and enters from the narthex, stands at the back of the sanctuary and rests against one of the ancient wooden pews. The choir is perched in a set of pews situated behind the main altar, fifty feet away, two rows of men and women moving their mouths in time with a man who waves his arms in front of them, without even a piano for accompaniment. Theodore closes his eyes and lets the sound they emit wash over him. The voices are filled with joy—two sets of voices it seems, the lower register singing a brief phrase followed immediately by an answering phrase sung by the higher register. He can feel the sound welling up within him, the vibration bouncing off the walls and across the taut receptive surfaces of his body. The words are hard to make out, at first—the tempo is fast—but he listens carefully and hears the repetition, the echoing phrases calling back and forth to one another:

For the instruments are by their rhimes.
For the shawm rhimes are lawn fawn
moon boon and the like.
For the harp rhimes are sing ring
string and the like.
For the cymbal rhimes are bell well
toll soul and the like.

The first phrase calling out in baritone, the second phrase echoing and answering back in the higher voice of the women, with a staccato emphasis on the final three words which repeat.

For the flute rhimes are tooth youth
  suite mute and the like.
For the bassoon rhimes are pass class and the like.
For the dulcimer rhimes are grace place
  beat heat and the like.
For the clarinet rhimes are clean seen and the like.

With his eyes closed he can feel the sound move back and forth across him and through him, he feels it register its tottering delight in satisfying and shapely stronger confinement across him and through him he feels it looking as if it were the body eternal the member of which is lost to sense is leaching through as a stream of balm is reverberating through all manner of depth as shaking through his body.

For the trumpet rhimes are sound bound
  soar more and the like.

For the TRUMPET of God is a blessed intelligence and so are the instruments in HEAVEN.

For GOD the father Almighty plays upon the HARP of stupendous magnitude and melody.

With his eyes closed still he in a passion dreams he is a leaping roaring with anything that passes through plummets through sounds in a witching way two thousand threescore and seven through arising forms and bodies shapes plucked from nothingness by angels in his head.

For at that time malignity ceases and the devils themselves are at peace.

For this time is perceptible to man by a remarkable stillness and serenity of soul.

With eyes closed this image's head is of fine gold this sound wrested within him a shout and whisper at his ear this heavy armor of vibration infiltrates and helpless he receives it painted on the inside of his head where silent dreams imagine forms and pull them out to something pulled and plucked to stand without complaint.

Hallelujah from the heart of God, and from the hand of the artist inimitable,

and from the echo of the heavenly harp in sweetness magnifical and mighty.

With eyes closed he sees the sound he feels it turn upon itself and translate all light into what it always has been, always has been merely sound, he feels the light in sweetness vibrate in accordance with the trembling touch every thing, even the orange light that filters through his eyelids, has become a variating key of vibration, a clapping shuffling baffling variance of sound.

"Okay, stop. *Stop.*"

The eyes are open again, the sound is gone. The man who was waving his arms has commanded it to stop. The voices of the singers have been flailed with a disparaging drop of the arms into mute silence, and the singers are left to stand and contemplate what it is they might have done to displease their master. Theodore cannot imagine what it could be. To him, this sound which still reverberates across the wood and plaster rafters of this tall and echoing space has seemed to be the very voice of wonderment, the type of sound he would imagine traversing the vast distances between the planets and their stars whenever he heard the archaic phrase: music of the spheres. He wishes it would never stop. But as the man stands there, stock still, staring at his charges, the last shred of their voices floats towards the rafters high above and dies away.

They wait with some patience to hear the indictments he will level at them, the description of their shortcoming, the instructions for what to do better next time. Perhaps the conductor is gathering his own thoughts, or letting them consider what they must know they have done wrong. The men of the lower register stand hunched together on the bottom two rows of pews—the women on the top two, a few men and women mingled together on the second row. And there in the middle of the top row, he sees the woman he knows, the one he met the other day—can it really be only yesterday?—at the coffee shop. She catches his eye, sees that he is staring at her, and smiles.

Theodore hopes the conductor, the choirmaster, doesn't see her smile and look back at him too. He wants to remain wholly anonymous, a pure transistor of these sounds and sensations, an unobstructed conduit through which they can flow.

The conductor does not turn his balding head around. He remonstrates them with the detached, resigned voice a parent would use to indicate that he is tired of having to tell his indolent children the same things over and over again.

"The timing is all off, people. Britten intended this piece to be call and *response,* modulating back and forth, and then coming together as one." One of his feet stamps down on the flagstones, just barely, a little tap, indicating his impatience. "This is an anthem, a song of praise and joy. So let's *hear* it—the sopranos are too *tight,* too tense. You're not blending. I want you to sound out, but I also want you to blend. You must sing your part and also come together—like this." And then the thin, balding, impatient man raises his arms in the air with his hands cupped, making two C's facing each other, like mouths emitting two competing voices, and he slowly brings the two hands together into one oval above his head and shakes it for emphasis.

"Now, *blend*."

In the moment before they begin again, Theodore looks around the nave of the church, the sanctuary. If there were such a thing as God, this would not be a bad place to meet Him. On each side of the long, resonant space, the cream-colored walls are punctuated by ribbons of lavender, gold, and orange stained glass, transposing the faint winter light from outside into a milky glow. At the point where the walls begin to arch towards the high central spine of the church, ribs of dark wood soar to the top of the vault, and as he looks at it from this vantage point, he sees why it is called a nave—it does look like the bottom of a large sailing vessel turned upside down and hoisted into the sky. Still, he can see a stain on the plaster there, another sign of leakage, decay, a roof in need of repair, neglected by an inner-city congregation dwindling in size and resources. This defect reminds him of the church his parents dragged him to when he was a boy, a less dramatic, modern building built in the plain, pedantic style of the sixties, which felt to him more like a cross between a supermarket and his elementary school, with its low flat roof, and its Sunday school lessons that felt like an unwelcome early intrusion of school work into his weekend.

As a boy, he would have liked to have believed the stories they were telling him about Jesus and about God—his mind had been certainly open to any kind of new knowledge—but the stories didn't seem to make sense, to hold together the same way the math and science lessons in his textbooks did. They seemed to be describing a world of magic and make-believe more akin to the fairy tales his mother used to read him when he was very little—slightly frightening in a way, because they invoked things that could not be seen or touched and often seemed to have a dire, foreboding twist at the end. A dutiful student, he had recited all the prayers and creeds they taught him, had admitted that he was born a sinner—though he never felt as if he really did anything wrong—in order to complete the confirmation class. He recited the words, but never felt they had any meaning—in fact, they seemed to have less meaning than the formulas in the trigonometry class he was acing in school. At least those words and symbols represented something in the real world, and he could manipulate them and make them do things that related to observable phenomena. The prayers and creeds in church seemed to be more a way for the Sunday school teacher and the droning minister to convince themselves that their jobs were important.

So once the confirmation ceremony was over, he rarely thought again about God, and he stopped going to church, except on special family occasions such as Christmas and Easter. Of course, he found the spectacle these holiday services provided to be moving, but more as a moment for family togetherness and a bittersweet reminder of the fleeting passage of the seasons—another Christmas together, another year gone by.

Now the choir is signing again, their words lifted up to the stained, overturned keel of the boat.

For the instruments are by their rhimes.
For the shawm rhimes are lawn fawn
moon boon and the like.
For the harp rhimes are sing ring

string and the like.
For the cymbal rhimes are bell well
toll soul and the like.

Theodore closes his eyes and tries to feel the same sensation he had a few moments ago, the sensation of the light behind his eyelids converting into sound, but this time it does not work. He is thinking about it too much. The sound is still wonderful, still pours over him like a round, flowing liquid, but it does not last.

For the flute rhimes are tooth youth
suite mute and the like.
For the Bassoon rhimes are . . .

"Okay, *stop!*" The choirmaster has dropped his arms again in disgust. "Everybody. You are not *together*. Just . . . take a break. Take ten minutes and come back and we'll try it again."

They file down from their pews that face the sanctuary from the altar, and the woman whose name he does not know heads down the aisle towards him, smiling to see him there alone in the big church with her.

"You came to see me!" Today, without the hats she was wearing and the green apron of the coffee shop, she seems smaller somehow, less aggressive. Her hair, which had been tucked up under the mesh of the one hat yesterday morning, drapes the sides of her head in a way that frames her face and softens it.

"You're good—I don't know why he keeps stopping you."

"Here, come with me. We only have a few minutes, and I want to show you something."

She takes his hand and leads him out the double doors at the back of the sanctuary, towards another door to the left as they enter the narthex, the large anteroom between the sanctuary and the front doors of the church. As she opens the door, he expects it will lead down, or into one of the many corridors he had been wandering earlier. Instead, it leads them directly to a small flight of stone stairs, no more than five or six, constricted within what must be the bell tower of the church. He follows her up the stairs and turns with her thighs just a few inches above him, turning and turning as they wind their way high up above even the peak of the roof of the church. He places his hand against the stone wall of the tower as they make each turn, to keep from slipping and tumbling down the stairs below.

At the top, there is a landing, and another small door to go through before they are out in the open on what feels like a platform high up in the sky, above the damp slate roof of the church, across from its green spire, above the blanket of black leafless trees spread out before them. They had climbed the steps in silence, and now, they stand next to each other, looking through the double stone archways at the view in silence. The amazing thing is how many trees there are even in this inner city neighborhood, filling the spaces between the woodframe houses, the black branches swaying gently, still months away from carrying their canopy of leaves.

"Isn't it wonderful?" The question she asks him does not require an answer. "I come up here sometimes after practice and just stare across the city for a while, close my eyes and feel the wind. I discovered the door was unlocked one day quite by accident—I thought it might have been a closet to hang up my coat!" Her face, the smooth skin of her cheek, is very close to him.

"That music—what was the piece you were singing?"

"Oh yes, it's Benjamin Britten, *Rejoice in the Lamb*. Quite a difficult piece really, for a little church choir like us. But the director, as you saw, is very ambitious. I like him for pushing us to try new things, beyond the basic hymns and psalms that everybody sings."

"It sounded like . . ." he has to search for the words, "a race to see who could sound more joyful."

His description makes her smile. "It's based on a poem by Christopher Smart, from England, in the seventeen hundreds. He wrote it while he was in an insane asylum." She turns her head to look at him. "They made him an outcast, put him in the asylum because he was falling to his knees in the middle of the streets of London, to worship God."

Her saying this makes him turn his eyes away from her and look out at the trees from the pinnacle of the church. He does not want to look at her and see what her eyes might reflect back at him, her clear gray eyes. He only wants to look out now, at the damp black blanket of trees and the scraps of white houses in between, and in the distance, beyond the arc of the lake where nothing is, the tiny blue green mirrors of the downtown office buildings poised like slices of cut glass about to fall down. He does not want to see anything that might see him back. All the parts of himself that made him what he used to be, the person whom he thought of as Theodore, have been washed away. He could stand here and watch over the trees and the houses for a very long time—the idea of time has no meaning for him now. It could be two o'clock in the afternoon or four thirty; what difference does it make? His sense of time has always been pinned on a sequence of appointments and projects and meetings and phone calls that are no longer there. In place of these things, there stands a vast blank nothingness, an empty space where the rest of his life waits for him to determine what it could possibly be. And because there are no more things for him to attach himself to, he has become merely a watcher of these trees, an empty blank something that stands here and feels the wind surge past, carrying with it a few stray drips of rain.

So perhaps, he thinks, time is only a man-made thing, a sequence of sensations that we convert into a stream of instants. The flow of one thing after another hitting our nerve endings. But we do measure it; we have created precise, technical instruments—clocks—built on the solid foundation of shifting gears or vibrating sub-atomic particles that can count out nanoseconds without fail for thousands of years. Still, he thinks, what are these clocks measuring but a sequence, a one by one pattern of the movement of objects, no matter how minuscule or how fast? Time can only be the change in the state of these objects, not something separate and unto itself.

His eyes blink, and he sees the trees again. He feels the presence of the woman beside him in the wind.

He does not want to be thought of as an outcast, like that dead English poet. He does not want to be thought of as insane. His mind has always wandered off as it did just now into purely conceptual things, wondering about how one thing relates to another, wondering about how the world he sees around him works and fits together. This has always been his strength as a scientist—his power of observation and the creative way he was able to translate the observations into abstract and mathematical frameworks. But somehow this talent seems to have ended up working against him. He somehow stepped over a boundary where others did not dare to go.

He looks at the woman and sees that she's been watching him think. Of course—this woman's face reminds him of what he has always known. This woman's face is what's real. The wind, the movement of air molecules across his skin, is what's real. Only the things he can observe are real, the solid, physical objects and their attendant motions. Everything else, the frameworks of thought and concept, the notion of anything beyond the particles, and atoms, and molecules—the idea of consciousness!—even the mathematical formulas he might use to describe the particles, none of that can exist outside of the pattern of electrochemical processes and charges flowing through the cellular structure of his brain. Those rational, clearheaded Englishmen had been quite right to throw that man, that poet, into an asylum.

More to touch another solid object than anything else, he turns and envelopes the woman's body in both of his arms. Feeling his arms around her, she turns more to face him, lifts her face up closer to his. Closes her eyes in anticipation of a kiss.

He keeps his eyes open and regards her face for a brief moment—her cheekbones are broad, high, Slavic perhaps. Her eyelids, even as they are stretched shut, are crinkled at the corners by fine, crêpey dimples where the skin shows her age. He can feel one of her breasts, cupped within his hand. It is larger, more full, than Ilene's. This, he thinks, is what's real. This woman's form, this body he holds in his arms. Nothing more.

He places his lips on hers and feels them yield. The sensation of two soft pillows opening up, wet, and then her tongue extending, reaching out—his tongue meets hers, searches, seeking attachment. While he kisses her, he thinks about what attracted him to her most, the beauty of a woman's collar bones poised beneath a clear smooth canvas of skin, more beautiful even than the breasts below, the intricate structure where the lines of the neck converge to the intersection where the chest is held taut, supporting the head and arms and shoulders—the crux. He thinks of this as his mind reaches out towards hers, his mind released from all other forms of attachment, released from everything that had made him who he was, now reaching out for something else to latch on to, out of panic, dread, and fear. There must be always some other thing, some other one to hold on to, something to reflect himself off of, to define himself by. And he thinks for a moment that this is what a woman is for—what Ilene has been and what this woman is now—a mirror, a prism, to reflect and refract himself off of. A perfect way to establish the form of his own self, to spur him on—that has always been Ilene's function—he would always view his own accomplishments through her eyes, thinking about how she would see it, what her reaction would be.

But what of that? It is all over now, and he has been avoiding going home to tell her because he cannot face the thought of letting her down. So here he is, betraying her, his mouth, his lips seeking the comfort of another woman, the thrill of attaching himself to this strange new person in his arms. In a way, this long kiss is more intimate, more of a betrayal than any other sex act could be, his face joined together with hers, the connection to her face more intimate than sex; for her mouth and face are closer to her brain, more uniquely hers alone, more significant of her individual nature than the genitals, which, though shocking and thrilling when encountered, are more generic, less indicative of the person with whom the connection is made.

Through this kiss, he is trying to define himself as someone once again. Not the blank emptiness he felt when he entered the church. He is Theodore: the failure, the betrayer, the experiencer of this woman's breasts and lips, and even that, though that is all he is and can be at the moment, is better than nothing. This kiss is what's real, nothing else. Not his old identity as a string theory physicist, not his marriage to Ilene, not his research grants or concepts about Perturbation Theory or his misguided musings about God. Those things are just ideas his mind needed to hold on to, to enable itself to say, "This is me, this is Theodore, this is who I am." But he knows now that the only true reality is what he can see or feel or hear or touch in this very moment—this woman's tongue drawing him near. That's all there is. Everything beyond her is only an illusion his mind has dreamed.

She pulls away from him. His hand is still cupped around her breast.

"I have to go back." Her eyes are blurred by what just happened. "Stay and we'll have dinner after."

"Yes," he says. "I would like that."

She turns to go down the stairs again, expecting him to follow, but he does not go.

"I'll just stay here for a while and look at the view."

She nods and is gone, her soft fragrant hair and small back receding down the dark passage, and even as she goes, he knows he will never see her again. He will never know her name. She will go on singing her beautiful songs, and he will do . . . what? He does not know. He has always been an ascetic—he would have made a good priest; he cannot allow himself too many attachments. He stares out over the churchyard and looks down at the dead yellow grass below. Today he has been relieved of nearly every attachment, every thing that held him to this earth. And this woman, just now, made him see how easy it is to latch on to something new, whatever comes along. If he had gone with her, he would only be building up another kind of Theodore, another identity, perhaps no better nor worse than the one that has been ripped from him today. So therefore, (he can see his mind working, like a kind of machine set out apart from him), therefore, perhaps it would be an apt and fitting test now to see what would happen if he tossed himself from the great height of this tower, from the top of this temple, to the frozen ground below. Would that not be the true and only test of whether he is only what he can physically see and touch, or whether there is something more? That is what a scientist would do, having formulated this hypothesis to test—and isn't this the only test that really matters?

What would happen next?

He has a sneaking suspicion that the one he has known as Theodore, the one who is thinking these thoughts, watching and deciding, would be no more.

No archangel would swoop down from the parapets to save him, or lift him up to heaven.

He would not be around to see what's next, so therefore, there could be no answer, no solution to this experiment.

And he cannot stand the thought, the vision that enters his head, which is the image of Ilene standing in the yard below surrounded by policemen and an ambulance there to take his lifeless body away.

THERE IS A garden on the way home. He has walked this way many times before, on his daily trek from the office building, across the north quad, towards the faculty parking lot. It is only a brief detour to pass through this nearly forgotten corner of the campus, a small garden tended with care in memory of an obscure benefactor of the university from the 1890s, the heiress of a soap-maker's fortune.

He turns into the garden now, marked at its entrance by two pinkish gray stones engraved with the name of the heiress. He has always coveted this out-of-the-way place, this corner of the campus not too many people know about or care to visit. He has always thought of it as his own private spot, where he could spend a few quiet moments in thought before the drive home, contemplating the beds of flowers blooming here a good part of the year. Today the beds are empty, the bulbs tucked beneath the frozen earth, dormant. Still, it has its beauty. There are two alleyways between the beds where he can walk, lined on both sides by giant sycamore trees, their wet black branches waving high above him in the wind. At the center of the garden is a desolate fountain in the shape of an octagon—the figure of the octave, of completion—out of which rises a green copper statue of Persephone, her gaze caught it seems between the underworld and the barren garden she watches over here above.

He knows he is only postponing the inevitable, dawdling here, as he has been doing all day long, wandering aimlessly, without direction or purpose. The sun takes a little longer to set in late February, but it is nearly dark by five fifteen. There is not much daylight left—soon enough he will have to tell Ilene. She will be expecting him home. He brushes his phone on to see if he has somehow missed a call from her. There are no messages, no notifications of an incoming call—only a handful of straggling emails, from colleagues who haven't heard the news of his demise, or those who copied him on routine notes out of habit or in response to a message with REPLY ALL. The world goes on without him, he can see. The emails still get sent, the science still gets done, and tomorrow morning the board meeting will still happen without him, and a new Research Director will be chosen to take Victor's place. He glances at the phone's tiny screen again and tosses it into the dirt. He won't be needing it any more.

At the end of the pathway, the garden bends away from campus and tucks against the side of a small hill, an unusual outcropping of earth where the terrain begins to rise a bit more steeply from the shore of the lake that defines the eastern edge of the city. Here, there is a strange relic from the original designers of this refuge—a set of concrete steps that leads down to a public restroom. The way in to this place is shrouded in shadow, with the sun dipping behind the knob of the hill; it looks like the entrance to a cave or a tomb. He takes the first steps carefully, not knowing what to expect. Seeing this place has reminded him that he needs to go to the bathroom, and he hopes the doors are open. That weak cup of coffee he had and the juice at the church are making him want to go.

The seven or eight steps that lead down to this enclosure smell of urine—not a good sign. Sure enough, the doors to both men's and women's bathrooms are bolted shut. And now that he has been thinking about it, he really does need to piss, urgently. He takes a quick look around, making sure no one can see him, drops his computer bag, unzips the front of his trousers, and lets fly. He can tell by the dank smell of this cavern that he isn't the first one who's done this.

After that bit of relief, his eyes have settled in to the gloom of dusk in this place. He looks around and sees dead leaves, a shriveled, desiccated condom, and, in the far corner, a bird's nest, falling apart, abandoned by old crows now forever gone away. Odd to find a bird's nest here in this low place—perhaps some animal dragged it down here or it was blown here by the wind. Would a bird seek shelter or find it in a place as far down in the ground as this? For all his knowledge of the physical mechanics of the universe at the grandest and most infinitesimal levels, his understanding of the natural world of plants and animals has always been lacking. He sets his bag down again next to the nest and kneels to take a closer look. It almost appears on closer inspection to be nothing more than a loose clump of grass and twigs, but he can see that it has been gathered together, formed by a being of some intelligence, into a coherent pattern, a slack, flowing weave of the bits of tree branch padded by softer brown grass in a semblance of a hollowed out circle not unlike a crown. The intent behind this crude undertaking—he pictures the black bird bustling about plucking these twigs and branches and weaving them together, purposeful, thoughtful almost—is comforting. At every level, life will find a means to survive. He turns and gazes up the steps at the wedge of sky above him, poised like a great gray stone that could wheel about and shut him in. He will rest here, lay his head down on the bag for a moment—only for a moment, he will close his eyes and rest.

The darkness feels divine. The backs of his eyelids are a perfect expanse of blankness, a field of nothingness where his mind can empty itself and go still. With his eyes closed and his other senses shutting down, he feels it—something hard in the briefcase his head is lying on. Not his computer, he left that back at the office in his hurry to get away. A book. His eyes open again and he sits up, unzips the front pouch where he sometimes puts a book or two he has been reading. He opens the hardcover book and flips through its pages—*The Mathematical Theory of Cosmic Strings: Series in High Energy Physics, Cosmology, and Gravitation.* He had been reading it on the flight to California, engrossed in its descriptions of infinite straight strings and loops and the associated singularity structures—the zero point and the infinite strings that go with it. Here, on page 337, is an interesting passage, something that had caught his eye:

"The remaining metric function, ψ, is fixed by the constraint equation (10.12) and can be expressed as an infinite series of toroidal harmonics. It turns out that ψ is well defined if ξ_0 is smaller than a critical value ξ_{crit} which depends only on the mass per unit length μ of the string. One interesting feature of the solutions, alluded to earlier, is that as $\xi_0 \to \xi_{crit}$ the ratio $M/(\mu L)$ of the gravitational mass of the string to its local mass tends to zero. Thus, the effect of the impulsive toroidal wavefront is, in some sense, to mask the far gravitational field of the string."

This had seemed to him to be an important insight into the basic structure of the universe, hidden here in the back pages of this obscure and mostly unacknowledged book. He had underlined the passage heavily in blue pen, in his typical manner of annotating books he reads, and had drawn a number of blue arrows in the margin pointing to the passage. The insight comes back to him—the image of a vast, infinite set of toruses spiraling out and away from an infinitely long string that spans the breadth of the universe—this could serve as the underpinning of the basic cosmic structure and the key to understanding the far-reaching, yet unexplainable effects of gravity. He turns the page to read more, and then *he sees*. There, buried in the back of the book, stuck between the pages, two folded pieces of notebook paper covered with his scratchings in blue ink—his notes! The notes he searched for everywhere; of course, how could he have not remembered. He had been reading the book on the plane, had gotten excited about this description of the gravitational effects of infinite strings, jotted something down on the notebook paper, folded it up and tucked it away. But his growing sense of panic at the hotel, his vision of doom, had blurred his thinking—he had searched everywhere in this bag, but didn't remember to look inside the pages of this book.

Here it is—the equation from the book that he jotted down in one of the few remaining spaces on his two pages of notes:

$$\psi_{,rr} + r^{-1}\psi_{,r} + \psi_{,\tilde{z}\tilde{z}} - \tfrac{1}{2}(\psi^2_{,r} + \psi^2_{,\tilde{z}} + \chi_{,rr} + \chi_{,\tilde{z}\tilde{z}}) = 4\pi e^{2(\chi-\psi)} T_{\mu\nu} n^\mu n^\nu$$

He had intended, on the plane, to refer to this equation and the idea of the toroids spiraling out from the infinite, universe-sized looping string, and the toroids masking the effect of the string's gravity, but he had been so totally flustered that he had forgotten all about it by the time he appeared on stage to give his presentation. And he had forgotten many other things, many other equations, scribbled in a kind of haphazard grid between the lines of the two pages of notebook paper. He looks at them now and remembers all the hours he put in, all the hard-fought victories and insights he had won and weaved into this research. All of it for naught.

Why couldn't he find these notes when he needed them? Why hadn't he sent them to himself in an email? That's the thought that worms its way into his head and will not go away as he lays the pages down beside him. He stares up at the grim gray wedge of sky. If there is a God out there in the heavens above, how could His will be so diametrically opposed to Theodore's own? How could God have wanted him to fail so miserably—in such an embarrassing way—by saying something to all those people about God? A kind and loving God would have wanted him to succeed, to make Himself known in a better way than this. But perhaps God is indeed the kind of vengeful, wrathful God Victor said he had no need for, when they were talking in his office. Theodore knows now why his colleagues had been so appalled by his evocation of God during his speech: We can only be certain of what we can see and measure and detect with our instruments and our own two eyes. Everything else is subject to guesswork and speculation, and the dangerous attribution of whatever any madman may want to propose as the Will of a Higher Being than us, without proof. In that case, there can be only the testimony of one man against another. When that happens, history has shown that the result must be bloody wars and tyranny and persecution, the very things that rational scientists and all sane men have been trying to rid the world of the past four hundred years.

Theodore closes his eyes and lays his head down again on his bag. Of course, there is no God. How could he have ever entertained such an idea? There is only the spinning, expanding remnants of an accidental explosion, shreds of energy that have slowed down enough after billions of years to congeal into clumps of cooling matter which exhibit a tendency to hang together in particular ways that sometimes allow for structures that show a slightly higher degree of order and self-perpetuation—what is commonly referred to as life. There is only the cruel cold vacuum of blackest space beyond this thin envelope of drifting clouds; there is only death and decay and destruction awaiting him and every other animal that has had the audacity to witness and consider the setting and rising sun, the infernal phases of the moon marching onward in its elusive transit across the sky. Into his head and through even his heart the pain of this knowing has spread, and with his eyes closed and his head sunken down upon the bag as a cushion against the hardened ground of the pit, he calls upon the mercy of sleep to calm him and send these terrible visions of affliction on their way.

And with eyes closed twelve corpses still across his vision fled, his field of vision still as wide as ever even with eyes closed images keep marching on. With eyes closed from thought his mind can image the stirred up relics of his very own soul, of the souls of every other man to regale with the visions that have contrived to arise and explore, that have stretched across whatever appears to have happened to one man and to all the rest, engendered in the head of one man and living for ever after in the heads of all who succeed. With eyes in rest he sees the cruel wings flapping of the swan, he reaches destinations every other man and woman have reached. With head in quietude his images can fly from one mass of glory to the next and he is free to match them thought for thought, free from shouldering the debt of first accounts and second. Free of civil gardens free from crimson pits and soldiering on for grieving joys of Job. In Gethsemane, all images are pressed out and forged together, from the shuddering loins of the earth, all desires are given their due.

Be gentle, for their souls are at work. Be kind, for creation is their power now and ever after.

In the belly of the beast, the mind has fountains of its own to deliver, has chasm spaces full of plots of gold; in the beast's blue belly, blue and dark and slippery and cold, the mind and soul conspire to generate their own Jonas delays, their own fine wet fountain spray of life ever-lasting. In the darkness still the brightness of the light inside can shine, the light which shined on shores of Genessaret, shines and grows. For kings are sometimes dwellers of the space within, and duchess loves cannot anchor down to sleep without a lack of light.

To have a dream, the prince must fall asleep and forget—forget that the dream is one with the dreamer.

Once forgotten, he can go inside the skull, he can dwell inside the nooks and crannies of the worn-down world in which he lives. The crown of skull can forge a proscenium arch, the sockets of the eyes are pot lights shining on a cast and plot he must undertake and bring to pass within. The cranium is as vast as any district, state, or nation, vast as treaties may declare, as any planet star or sun, and within it by agreement will be overflowing with the fullness of imagination, images that are nothing but his own whether they are against his heart and eyes or whether they are for them.

Song, song, song; no God was seen nor heard, no staring equanimity with eyes that rot like fruit left out too long on a grocer's shelf, ears of no congratulation, never thrown a solitary sound. No God was seen nor heard. Only the objects of the worn-down world, the collected experience of two million years of mankind thrown open to roil and boil like a pot full of wretched refuse, all pressed down and shaken together. Waves of crying bright self-aroused and broken enemies, a furnace of heat and falling planet toil, to hear them talk, to arrive with sailors setting forth from shores to a destiny unknown and unforeseen, two extraordinary jointed travelers, Jason setting forth with his hands tied against his night of woe, encumbered in the belly of the ancient wooden ship, dominion over the waves of leaping tall and weeping in the eager moonlight swell, the wetting world of water all around, slapping against the belly of the ancient ship. Out-setting against all sanity and odds led forth by the promise of only hauling a golden catch, every night he sets forth over rain-sodden waves, on against the immense expanse of watery every where the depths of its ocean-tide more frightful than the width extending to forever. What lies ahead can surely be no more filled with dread than what lies beneath—what pushes up against the shifting creaking dry rot hull beneath his feet: the sum of all the million years of human kind all pressed down and stirred together:

   Snakes cut down from their fetters, released from their trees, the annual sum, the tortured tonic mysteries, mothers and fathers torn from their children, children torn from their silver victories, river banks and dunghills, shades against a midnight glare, accountants, defendants, attendants, repressible whores and slayers of infidels, founders of empires long since turned to dust. Here they all are, distilled into a paste of dreamy longing:

   Fall roses, clinging to one final dying breath of muffled doom, a squire traveling, with a troupe of his own companions, an artful parade of children's toys lined up and waiting to be jested, shoes and boots and other rags of clothing, discarded and disused, cracked ceramic plates and crockery, the translucent wings of bees. City streets and vistas over avenues in towns that no longer exist, houses shuttered and houses gleaming new on the first day someone entered and called them home. Old discarded tools and archaic ways of speaking, words in languages that no one ever speaks, methods of writing with chisels and feathers and parchments, alphabets that no one can decipher, symbols that mean nothing to anyone any more. Here they all are:

The eyes of a woman who was someone's mother, someone's wife, the lips of a child who spoke her name, both of them dead and gone. Species of leaving creatures too numerous to count, who swam and ran and flew across the waters and the plains. A tourniquet, a guillotine, a gas mask and a neoprene defender and invader. Shell casings and powder horns, arrow tips and battering rams, hot oil poured on the heads of someone's children, five pounds of lead blown through the chest of someone's father. Organ pipes and catgut strings, rough-hewn canvas and paints made out of oil. Loose-bound leather books that hang together sewn by hand.

Sparrows and harrow rows for turning up the soil, lions and plumb lines for plotting out the beam, here in Golgotha's cranium cave they are stirred and boiled together.

And across the still hoar frost of the night that bears its weight upon the pit in which he lays, above the garden's sleeping shadows deep, his soul traverses and surveys, consummates the journey every soul must make across the giant chasm void each night, concentrates the faint impressions of the day into a seascape vast and ever rearranging. The waxing yellow disk of the moon shudders and peeks above a bank of cloud, tall and shifting through the freckled burning early morning stillness and cold; the wind raises up from the shores of the lake, propelled by the gradient of warmer air above the liquid mass and sucked around the darkened storefronts and apartment blocks, behind the towers of the campus quad and slinking through Persephone's shadow, her arms out stretched, palms down, her blessing granted to the earth her winter home, the wind creeps down the stairs into the pit where his ancient dreaming head lays sleeping, streaming its cold wet breath into his ear.

So therefore, the dreams go numb, the giant ship pauses atop the crest of a wave, settles its weight there and its admiral surveys the vista vast and deep. Tied to the mast, bound and gagged against the call, the dove's tail slithers through the clashing rocks, the potion casts its spell. The golden object of desire slips away, its fine and wispy wool unravels and disavails. Having met with no disaster other than his own creation, his head is free to bolster yet another day. Jesus never knew what hit him in the end. They dragged him off the cross and tossed him in the tomb. But when he woke again to find that one life ends and so soon after another one begins, he announced himself as if nothing happened, nothing but the coming of another day.

Another day the sun rolls round, the earth spins spirals round the moon. The pallor of the first dim rays exposed, the shining glory grows to be indemnified. They pried him off the cross and when he raised himself again they wondered who this new man was, when he dared to bear his golden fleece before them, golden halo round his head, they stood before him, shocked to see his countenance again. For they said, he is beside himself, he who wakes and dares to show his face again with each new breaking dawn.

THE PHONE IS still there in the dirt where he threw it the night before. Even being outside on the frozen ground the whole night hasn't hurt it—these gadgets are virtually indestructible now. A few months before, he had left this very same phone in the pocket of his favorite pair of jeans, and Ilene had tossed it in the wash. Too late, he thought, one complete rinse cycle must be enough to knock the life out of it. But Ilene said "Quick, put it in the freezer. I heard that will dry it out."

Sure enough, the phone had pulled through then, and a full night of bitter cold could do nothing more to hurt it now.

Thirteen more email messages have found their way into his inbox since yesterday evening, the last time he checked, even though he no longer works at the Institute. And six new voice messages. Two from Victor and four from Ilene. He can imagine what they must be—Ilene wondering where he is around six o'clock, late for dinner; Ilene growing concerned by seven when she hadn't heard a thing. Ilene perhaps calling Victor and Victor calling him. Ilene again and Victor again, then Ilene growing frantic, having heard the news about his job, and Victor worried too. Worried enough to offer him his job back? He doubts it, but he doesn't want to hear the messages, doesn't want to hear the fear in Ilene's voice. So he hits the green button to dial and taps the quick dial icons that call home.

On the second ring she answers, hoping it might be him.

"Hello?" Her voice is ragged from lack of sleep. "Theodore—where are you?"

"I'm okay. I'm sorry, I should have called, I found my notes and laid down to rest . . ." How can he explain it. "And I guess I just . . . shut down."

"I told Victor to call the police—they were all over campus and the neighborhoods around there looking for you. They said if you didn't turn up by morning they would start dredging the lake."

"I'm sorry, I just . . ." His voice falters—there really isn't any explanation. He has news to tell her. "Listen, Ilene, I figured out what happened. I know who did it."

"Did what?"

"I know who sent that message, the email that went out to everybody with my notes in it—the notes I wrote the other night. That's what got me fired—that email. Didn't Victor tell you?"

"I guess so. He told me he had to let you go—the Chairman of the Board told him he had to fire you. He didn't say why except it was because of the thing that happened out in California."

"Well, it's not just that—it's a long story. The other night, after the symphony, I had a dream, more like a vision really, and it gave me some ideas that I wrote down. I usually email my notes to myself, *so I don't lose them!* Can you believe it? I didn't want to lose these notes, and then that bastard Pradeep has been getting in to my email, and he sent them out to everyone. See, he must have gotten my password when we've been working on the Plasma Dynamics project together—what a dumbass I've been, using the same password for my server account *and* my email, the kids' names crunched together. But that sonofabitch saw these notes had some ideas about consciousness in them and he sent them out to everyone and their brother, everyone on the Board and at the Institute and everyone who was at the conference. And when the Chairman saw that, he freaked."

"Wow."

"That bastard Pradeep. He knew exactly what he was doing." Theodore is walking at pace now, leaving the garden. Walking with a purpose. "Listen Ilene, I'm going to the Board Meeting and I'm going to tell them."

"Tell them what?"

"Tell them that Pradeep did this."

"What good will that do?"

"I don't know, but I have to do it. I have to say my piece. At least I can try to clear my name, tell them these were my personal journal notes, not something I intended everyone to see. This is how a creative scientist has to work. It may not be conventional, but you need to think outside the box sometimes to come up with new ideas. And then that bastard will have some explaining to do himself, right there in front of Victor and the Board."

Nothing comes back to him, no response. Then, "I guess so. What have you got to lose?"

"You're damn right. Best case, I convince them to give me my job back. Worst case, it throws a giant wrench into rubber stamping Pradeep for Victor's job."

"Are you sure about this? Maybe just wait and talk to Victor. Tell him in private and let him tell the Board."

This is why he didn't want to call her right away yesterday. She doesn't understand the way things work around the Institute, and he didn't want to have to explain everything to her without having time to think.

"No, I've got to do this—what time is it? I have to go."

"Ten after eight."

"Okay, good, plenty of time." He does the calculation, probably ten or fifteen minutes to get across campus and up to the ninth floor conference room. He can make it if he hurries.

"I have to go, I have to hustle over there."

"Why don't you just come home?"

"I have to do this. I was supposed to be at this meeting, and I'm going to be there. I'll call you later."

Already with this first brief phone call, he feels as if he has been sucked back into the grid of his old life again—people making demands of him, people telling him what he should do. Time feels compressed again; once again he is running late. As he hurries across the pavements that lace the northwest corner of the sprawling campus, he wonders whether it might be better to go back to that path he was on yesterday afternoon and keep on walking. Walk away from everything that has bound his old life together, the phone calls, the emails, the expectations. He considers those several hours of absolute freedom he experienced yesterday, how the world had opened up into a vast blank gray abyss. This has often been a fantasy of his, to run away somewhere on his own, a lonely cabin in the woods far from any other person, surviving on very little food, reading books and writing down his musings by whatever light the sun provides, no phone, no computer, no television—maybe a select few CDs for music; he cannot do without his music. But it would probably grow old quickly, a week or two at most. Maybe all he really needs is a very long vacation.

Still, there was something lovely about the way his senses had released themselves from their usual pattern of knowing, unconstrained by the relentless headlong tumble of his thoughts. Already here in the midst of the first wave of half-awake undergrads straggling towards their morning classes, he can feel the pinch of his old familiar world closing in on him, his status as a member of the faculty readily accruing to him by virtue of his age and the rumpled clothes he wears.

On the frozen tarmac path ahead, angling across the maze of quads bound by limestone walls, he has a sudden memory of his daughter, gone away to live a life of her own, laughing at one of the overworked jokes he used to tell, her head tossed back, advising him that his jokes were all meant for third graders, but laughing just the same.

Forgive me please, he would say to her now. Forgive me for not holding on to every moment like that even as it was happening. For soon enough those moments evaporate and fade away. The clock ticks and the earth revolves into whatever it is that comes next. And the moment is gone.

Heading north towards his old office, he could just as easily be slogging to work again today the same way he had the day before. The buildings of the campus are just as beautiful as they have been every other day, the sky half filled with clouds, a bank of them pressing low towards the lake and shredded there, ripped into drifting loose curls of gray fluff by the wind. If he had it to do over again, he would have devoted less time to work, would have never come in on a Saturday morning, foregoing a day at the park with the kids for a few more hours staring at the whiteboard and the computer screen and the scribbled equations there that are gone now, all gone. In the midst of the students and their hangovers on the way to class, he can feel himself dwindling to a single solitary point, alone. The kids are gone, his son and his daughter, their laughter only an echo in his ear. His work is gone, the years of research, and with it any sense of worth he could bring home to Ilene. He is only now a point of dim awareness, taking in a shifting set of images brushing past him as his legs carry him one foot and then the other in the direction of the giant building that looms against the sky, hanging over him just ahead as if it were a mountain, one last mountain left to climb.

Inside, he takes the elevator to nine. The elevators are wedged into one of the many weird angles the new modern section of the building has after having been grafted on to the older ivy-covered limestone hall. But there is a spacious waiting area and a reception desk as he steps out, with wonderful floor to ceiling windows providing a panoramic view of the campus. There it is, all spread out before him. All of it his once. He had been part of this, a respected pillar that helped prop all of this up. The students move across the quad gracefully, in slow motion it seems from this height, threading their way towards their own destinies, making their own way in a world that no longer exists for him.

Wait. A voice somewhere in a corner of his brain calls out. This can all still be his. He can go to the meeting and tell them—tell them what Pradeep has done—and they will redeem him. Of course they will! He is too valuable to be cut loose. He is an important part of the work here. That's been part of the problem these past few days—he hasn't stated his own case strongly enough, hasn't stood up for what's rightly his. They can't just take it away from him. He has devoted his life to this place. He has given it everything he has to give. He looks down on the mellow lumps of limestone and the quads still brown in winter and the black trees etched against them and the students weaving their way through them and knows he can have it all back, he can do this. Just a word, the right word, spoken at the right moment, can make it all his again.

It is a short walk down a wide hallway, a gallery really, of empty conference rooms with walls of glass. The one he wants is the largest one, at the end of the corridor. Each of these rooms is like a fish bowl surrounded and defined by glass, their inhabitants visible for all to see. He stops outside and sees the room full of people, many of whom he knows, and the sight of him freezes them for an instant, the ones who don't have their backs to him. There is Pradeep, his eyes wide, watching him with the same look Thomas must have had, seeing him stand before them again, back from the dead. There are several of the Board Members, half a dozen of them on one side of the room who can see him through the glass, with the Chairman at one end of the table, wondering why he is here. And there is Victor at the other end, staring at him, his eyes pinched down to a glare, gesturing with one hand touching the other, about to make a point, and wondering whether Theodore will simply continue to stand there as a spectator, a witness to what is happening, or whether he will have the audacity to actually come into the room among them.

Theodore does go in. He watches them for a moment longer, frozen there in a tableau, a group of men gathered round a table in a painting; he approaches the glass door and opens it and enters. Then there is a moment, the moment of his ultimate power, when all eyes are on him standing before them in one corner of the fish bowl as it were, even the eyes of those who had their backs to him, who have turned to see what the others are staring at—who has entered the room?

And Theodore can see now what he couldn't have understood yesterday or the day before: They have brought someone in from outside! Theodore is not the only reason Pradeep has a look of shock and anguish on his face. There, on the righthand side of the room, among the women and men who had their backs to him, is the outsider, a Russian physicist named Rainer Milshovsky—half Russian, half German now that he thinks about it—the director of the program at the University of Moscow, who could be here for no other reason than to take Victor's job. That's the one thing Pradeep and Theodore could not consider in their closeness to the situation and to each other, that the Board might actually dare to go to someone outside the Institute—they had been so busy trying to jockey for position between themselves, and Victor had never given them any reason to believe otherwise, and now here he is, Rainer, sitting between Amanda and the Chairman looking already like he owns the place.

It could be that they have brought Rainer in as the token of a thorough search, to mollify the Board and maintain all sense of propriety that all available qualified candidates have been considered. There had briefly been talk from Victor of wanting to hire a woman, or some other minority candidate, but in their many discussions over lunch in the student union or in the narrow enclosure of Victor's office, Victor had always assured Theodore that he had the inside track. The look of pure shock and despair on Pradeep's face confirms it—the Russian is in.

Victor breaks the spell. "Theodore, it's good to see you. I'm glad you're okay." This last is said without a trace of malice towards the interloper in the midst of their party. But then Victor does have to ask the question everyone is thinking as they stare at him.

"What do you want?"

The revelation comes from the question. Theodore scans the room and then his eyes go towards the far wall, also floor to ceiling glass, with a broad expanse of sky on the other side. From behind a shred of cloud, a single ray of sun erupts, glances past and imparts to the cloud a celestial outline of golden filigree. And there, beyond the golden cloud, a single star shines halfway up the sky from the horizon—or could it be a planet? It is still close enough to daybreak to see the star trembling there, its light flickering against the gray backdrop of the morning. He closes his eyes and the light from the star approaches, the light from the star fills his vision, fills his head and he sees it as a worshipping of the star in the east in the chambers of his imagery, the star of morning and the sun combining, the star of morning fills his vision as a single eye. The secret vision of the spirit thrust his sword in the fellow's side to open the star everywhere to seek what's inside and also afar off the star brought near enough to touch, the star which is fallen down from heaven into his open sword wound and his open single eye, the star which grows beyond his secret vision to encompass all and all, with colors blooming from points of color dying daily, point of orange grows to red and green and blue, point of blue enthralls to purple, pushes open leaves of violet and magenta, octave pushing up and out to the eye between the brow and through the crown beyond the head, the thousand-petalled canticle, the hymnal lingers at the door to seek what's inside and afar off, the star that opens everywhere encompassing all and all. Trembling literal raise a whisper of light of perishable undaunted violent light to the heavens from within exploding outward through the star that's fallen from the sky and flowing once again through the body through the coursers and the rivulets and channels of the body through the lovely luxury clean replies of petals at each crossing whom the light belongs to wrapped up and from every candle rippling petals flickering the light progresses up and out and back through the body to the heavens once again. Be the star that he is one with it, with points and spheres and whirls of color dying daily. Be the light and behold it—for beyond the light is only the source of the light. And the source of the light is only he who is. Why lament the light and the source of the light when he is one with it, why suffer being separate and apart. He allows to be open the thousand petals thousand doors to every myriad channel and the light pours through him, directs from violet into white. The whiteness of all colors and all sound, the blessed chord of all vibrations all notes sounding together and at once, turning light into color into brightness into blossom abstract absence of substance torrents bursting out of breathing into sound all white and bright and standing in the middle of the sun there is no feeling left, there is only empty whiteness and a terrible savage tearing sound which is the absence of all notes because they all become as one. This is the perfect point where all wishers wants are washed away, the circle point, the diameter circumference and center all in one. From unity there is no need, there is no angle to perceive. From oneness one whole note the prayers of the saints are whispers undenied, from one and only sound the exhibition of another angel with a golden censer floating and sinking can only perish exposed until it is no sound at all. From one whole and only light, there is no more singing, no more dance, there is only tapestry of white. The circle point, the center golden white, the source of every light. I am, in a word, in an instant, I am the point and the circle which is perfect every where and no where all at once. I am here and there, which is singularity and infinity and every moment locked into one, the circle and the point which knows no bounds, which knows and loves and is. I and he and others never wasn't, we will always be. The moment of beginning is a dreadnaught moment without end. The only every many one of whiteness and dazzling triumph cornets from the heavenly harp magnifical and mighty. The thousandfold and billionfold and myriads of millions of conspirators of particles of light are only really sound the single sound that made the ravening the rending falling out on the earth, are really only one sound that precipitates and propagates through whatever promise of joy could hold itself together long enough to love. There is only one, there is only I me I he I we am are he is I am us. There is only white bright sound light spell forth twanging single sound chord note behold bespoke to forthwith hold the white bright flagrant flashing light sound noise that's twanging back and forth behold the earth. There is only what he is and only what he is being through his seeing solid sea of sound.

Through his hearing solid spectacles of searing light. Through this one and only antiphony of sacred bliss, insomuch as he is and it is and there is only it, he is delivered to a glorified is and only is, he is pouring out his vial to the only vessel which can receive it, sending it out unto himself. He is and only that which is can be him. Can pour it out and send it unto himself and receive it. And then, behold a new thing. A second thing, an other thing. A seed of thought, a grain of sand that grows and grows, propelled by nothing more than the authority of his thinking. The word came forth, the thought that gives rise to everything in form is nothing more than the idea that there is separation, there can be more than one. Blessed is the man, the voice which gives authority to the word, and blessed is the thought, which is not a chastisement nor a blasphemy, blessed is the thought which moves the one into the many, for the one must know itself and feel the force of movement through the growing burgeoning wideness of the more than one. So—a seed of thought that grows and grows and here now everything erupts and goes out and on and fathers outward a cup filled with separation, lamps made precious with griefs with roared and roaring bosom secret places perfect decomposition slumping outward from perfection ignorable only here now everything explodes and goes on and exhilarates here now declare ye here how now goes out from past which is the one to future which is many, here now he is blown down to his knees with roaring through his hearing ears with seeing through his searing eyes here he on his knees is blown down as everything is trumpeted and shouted out and on and on, word thought deed word on reel and fisher soul of vast and shamed battalions mountains majestic presence [shall return shall set forth] his image his aura injured his misery priceless and precise his alarm his etheric body and his every age and [plaything] and signal flame and retribution for his spirit and out and on it goes his everything explodes and dissipates and blasts itself onward as he sinks down to his knees his nostrils shrank his gazes through his Horus eyes are open and nations declaring and passage over seas and twilight liveries his flannel sweating through his shirt his trumpet call, his strings his keys and notes of the harp of stupendous magnitude and melody the red key the golden tannin beauty of the bottle, therefore on and outward he goes exploding and blasting onward from one thought that there is me and there is what is not me bursting forth from nowhere which is he: go set forth and propagate initiate and boil and burn, bait beyond the spiral exposition is expounding [shall gladly lead and instigate] and declare an adamant rejection of true sight and knowing go on and get ye hence go hear ye this O priests and hearken for there is only all the songs of things that bursting forth from him are: cash brow self-made startling soaring open air, are heart and mind and body, are certain joys and sycophants, are heavenward ridiculous inceptions, are rounding and resounding grapple calls strapping themselves besides the sky, are bosom untended and denying, so hear ye this O priests for wherewith undertaken in the exploding mysteries of light are many things [acolytes and Orion catbird calls] shall gladly lead and instigate, and all this is one moment, one instant wherein he has been driven to his knees by sound and light and many things exploding from the night, from his dreams and visions all distilled through the five-pointed beauty of the star in morning bright, from the oneness with the only one and separating from the point and riven radius circumference. Driven to his knees his singing sound is resounding through him, his light and blessed heavenward inception calls a madness through him, clarion reception in a private point of starry pearl of light. And they said to him—wherefore art thou a madness and a madman—they say to him the one at the head of one end of the table and the other at the other end—first "What do you want?" then "What are you doing?" Then, he answered, if only in his mind [behold thy servant.] And he that seeketh findeth; and to him that knocketh it shall be opened, if only in his mind. The book of revelations is a secondary symptom of a madman; only those who are insane can know beyond the solipsism of this world. And in a dim corner of his madness he hears them asking, hears them filter through the on-rushing explosion of the sound. [What are you doing?] Singing, living, knowing. Opening all the way to joy. Shouting out in pure preciseness piercing pain. Be gentle, for their souls are at work. Open all the way to joy. Song, is singing, song, song, song. Be kind, for creation is also their power now and ever after. He knows now that to have a dream he must fall asleep and forget that the dream is one with the dreamer. He must have fallen asleep like all the others here and now he sees them sleeping [while he is singing]. While he is awake now what was rejected becomes the corner-stone the basis and foundation of a mighty edifice he is awake and he is pure light as thought transcending bursting forth through him as song vibration through infinity channeled through as one resounding call and response antiphony, the call is I am and the response is that I am, crucified and slain the courses of the luminaries of the heavens egress logic was asleep with nervous silver handicraft might control to Urizen to cloud-tracking holders-on with rolling lures direction precipice with heavenly eyes of Horus the gazers no particular life to suffering to Zion to blaspheme with the celestial city with the all-seeing one the solitude through changeful courage and eternity, he calls them by their names he savors as an ointment poured forth with invisible and dignified and decomposed with weeping sought the bare beginning famous for life a crown redeemed. I am light which is spirit which is energy which is projected through a screen of thought which is the idea of pure form which is as an angel standing in the sun and refracts the light into forms which manifest and express into the world of physical frozen light slowed down into objects manifest and beholden to the Lord. And the Lord is the Law of Laws which describes the forms and functions of the objects and the litanies of all the heavens and all the earth, in which way they must congregate and hold together and bear all within the bosom of their forms, which is the King of Kings, which is the Theory he sought and treasured in his days, the Lord of Lords. The Law of Laws decries that all things must turn back upon their maker, all things are emitted by their thoughts and forms through energy of spirit which is light of consciousness which is all, and refracted through the holographic screen of pure form idea they must remit and propagate and hence forth disintegrate and turn back unto their maker. So knowing this decrees it, showing this belies it, misunderstanding this is only one way to deny it. The Lord of Lords is and all ways will be was. He sees that all is thought and all is light, the King of Kings is a giant thought which came forth and always is and he is always part of it. And as a giant thought triumphant holds together cleaves unto itself, which is what he has known as Gravity, pulls itself together always any part of it is held unto the one. And as the Lord of Lords is and always will be a giant thought composed of light, all things are made of light and traverse from one point to the next in the self-same always instant, so there is no time there is only separateness of thought or unity of thought, and the degree of separateness of thought decrees how far apart the one thing is from the many, how long ago or in the future is the deed. With thought and in thought the one can travel across the vastness span of light in the selfsame always instant so traversing future past and present into now, so transgressing here and there and every-where into one. With thought and in thought most thoughts are directed into otherness and into separated forms and so they are dreams of a myriad of forms a thousand thousands and ten thousand times ten thousand, and all these forms are of necessity a promulgation and transmission of the light of thought as in a dream. And dreams dissolve and dissipate when the dreamer wakes. All dreams resolve and withdraw again into the mind the consciousness of the dreamer. So while he is awake now the dream is resolved and the only pure vision is sound vibration light of conscious spirit [while he is singing] through his body resonating with the one true light which is the Lord of Lords. And he sees now that the first forms are the simplest and they are spiral toroids whirlwinds of light twisted around upon itself and always spinning in one direction or the other up or down around or across and these are the first and basic parts of transgression physical transmission and as above so below, so all things partake of this basic formula and forging format. A human body spins and whirls with the same design as the selfsame particles that form it, for they are all projected, as above and as below, with light through the identical imaging and holographic screen. Encompass the breath of spirit, endeavor to unfold within a sheath light slowed down enough to pull together as a bright and insubstantial whirlwind of matter, the first-slung fouling come-together of glory. This is not the first time he has awakened and seen that the Lord of Lords is this: the Law of Laws is everything is rendered unto itself, everything unto itself is rendered. This is not the first time he has been awake and seen the Duat the Qa'aba the celestial chamber the lofty ones the eye of Horus the opening of the mouth and the shaking of the earth, the horn of the hidden place watched over by the phoenix bird which is the stairway to heaven. His name was given once when he did not die a second time, he has awakened not only once but a thousand times. Everything is expelled and whirls about and turns about and is rendered unto its maker. This is not the first time he has seen his lives and who he is and has been and will be all the same. He was a priest of Akkad and Shumer once he was a tailor in Chaldee he counted bales of wheat he will be a father of a glorious sun, he dried date palms and stomped on plains of withering mud in the ancient kingdom of Sesonchusis. On Saturn once he lived as a spirit intermediary between his lives on earth, his mind expressed in colors green and tan and blue, his love endowed with crystal flowers of methane and his wisdom flowed like winds through channels curling and unfurling at a thousand miles an hour. He bore a child once in Ur and died in the bearing, in ancient Armenia he scaled the highest peak and witnessed the cavern remains of the Double Doors of Heaven, his name was given once and he rose upon the steps of Light the red eye of Horus rising through the eastern midnight, he lived as a creature barely awake through many pasts and lifetimes living his droning stately and motley lives unaware of what they might have meant, these lifetimes hereby accounted only dim and distant memories and glimpses down a mirrored hall. A meal of roasted horse flesh gathered up from the dirt floor of a wooden hut on the plains of Scythia, a life as a leather tanner in the precincts of Adana and the Cilician Gates. He died as a child and in childbirth many times, he died as a young girl slashed and hacked by marauders, he died as an old man in the precincts of Zwickau, in the land of Thuringia died then in his sleep, and all of these lives were lived half asleep doing things going places, moments of song and dance moments of despair but hardly recognized and barely remembered after death, for he was not awake then. And also there were other lives many others when he knew, he woke and was awakened and he caught himself without falling, he rose up and is risen. A life one hundred and seventy eight thousand years ago in a land whose name he has forgotten and has been wiped away from history, a language lost to eternity he spoke and taught others to speak, he wrote it down on parchments and kept it safe within the halls of a temple whose pillars and beams have turned to dust. He was awake then and he knew the Law of Laws that everything is rendered unto itself. He lived many short lives and several of them in China and others in America thousands of years before it was called that, and he was awake in those lives and saw his former and future selves, in one of those lives he was a teacher, in several of them he was a slave not knowing half-asleep, in one of those short lives he lived as a merchant selling wine in the ports of Santander and Gijon. He never left some places traces of his spirit there remain, he went back to several times and places and lived with his other selves there again and again. In India he died once or twice or a hundred times, the lives spread before him are too numerous to count. The lives and births and deaths spread out before him like a tapestry of knowing and unknowing, motion pictures that are more than films, that are lives he could slip into and exist within again if he chose. All the languages he ever spoke too numerous to count: Hebrew, Persian, Syriac and Ethiop, Armenian and Akkadian, and Old Church Slavonic, Greek and Saxon and Roman and Manx and languages whose names and sounds are lost and forgotten and have not yet been spoken. He performed the designs, he has felt every emotion joy and love and fear there is to be felt, he wore on his head the celestial disk. Spread before him even are his future lives—he has raised himself so high enough to see them. They keep on going, they never end. He calls to himself and to himself responds. He leaves these lives behind. And the Lord has sent him to Beth-El and to Cambyses where the water is so weak that nothing floats upon it, and he sees a great end and in turn a great beginning for what was selected is cast away, what was rejected becomes the corner-stone of a mighty edifice. The stumbling block becomes the rock, the foundation upon which he reaches and raising himself up he has not answered them, he sees further, beyond his own lives and the lives of others, out and onward and beyond. He has raised himself up as if to float upon it, though nothing can float upon these waters, he is receiving now, for everything that can exist is in the image of the beholder. He has all time before him now he drinks from the stream of eternity and has passed by Zotiel who guards the gates, he has raised himself up to the summit of the mountain that reaches to heaven and the treasuries of the stars, he has all eternity before him. And his name was raised and his spirit, and he raises himself and the angels raise him. And he looks and sees stone and star and earth receding and all the tapestry of lives receding so he sees the luminaries of the stars in the east in their courses towards the sun and the luminaries in their courses to the heights of the darkness beyond and these are as lights cast before him as stones and pebbles in a garden, and he is lifted up to see the culminating arms and centuries and their dawn of treasure sent across the gulf beyond the regions of heaven known to man. The word of the Lord comes and electrified and with only his name and his spirit he raises himself up to beyond the stars of heaven bound together for there are cycles beyond the stars and their worlds, at the place where the stars are bound together gates are guarded by tongues of light and slipstream vehicles to deny the blight of missing currents for there is a blackness at the center which denies all everything who enter. Beyond the blackness are cycles beyond the vanities of flesh, drawn within and higher still than any luminaries in the regions known to man. And even as he has drawn himself here he sees the other men who watch him [their eyes projecting what they choose to see] their eyes projecting tubes of vision of their local cramped and building world, they see him as a horror and he sees beyond what they will ever [choose] to know/ here there is a circle of cherubim with feet of burnished bronze with sickened and holy smiles to welcome whom they watch, here the wicked dare not tread the weary wanderer may come to dread the boiling treaty of his faith in form and physicality dissolves and dissipates and he sees it terraced and carved up into the screen from which it is projected overlaid with a swastika pattern of creased and cruciform grid, which is the screen of holographic projection, which is the pure form of idea laid over the light of spirit which infuses every thing. It sickens him and frightens him. When he is high enough and within enough now, the images he sees are beyond celestial and also still within this room and he sees the conference table and the faces of the men who look at him in horror dissolve into a cruciform swastika grid which overlays them, the whole conception of this time and space is seen by him as only something as if it might be a pixelated holograph projection without himself to do the direction /[they call for help he horrifies them so/] when he is high enough now and within enough he sees them dissolve and he is in the black space where the stars have come together, and he sees that every star is an entity, a being not unlike himself but of greater cohesion and magnitude, their coursers and their columns of light are like their limbs and pillars marching across the sun, their spirits and their names are famous creases of roiling light contained and compressed into brilliance and they come together now and then to burst forth into another life. Forsaken in the black space there are cycles above and beyond, cycles and heavens beyond spaces and times he could ever hope or dream to imagine and the only archers and singers and bidding to become is the constant Law of Laws which even here is judging and supreme, the Lord of Lords conceives of even this and defines it, which is everything unimaginable sacred and profane. For these cycles some of which are darkness for darkness is as necessary as light for darkness is only the space which light has filled and seeing the darkness means he is the light that fills it, for these cycles some of which are desperateness and derision for he sees there the transform of effect the pure form and foundation of physical laws, the Theory that operates on the lower level from which he has come. For these cycles are the circuits of heaven spiraling up and up and within and in and ever inward and onward and unto their courses and their cycles there is never any end. So therefore there is only himself to chastise and revise and ever inward he is drawn as outward and beyond the celestial disk he goes, and so therefore in the blackness and pure light his images are washed and torn away floods and history and crosses sheared of water hills and dread and shaking ground and music and perfume shaking trembling washed and torn away, pious land ploughed away and furrowed through the ruts on the plain and on the mount, on Capernaum and Galilee it sings through him even as it dissolves. There is a song that he is singing even as his every sense and image is washed and torn away, which is everything unimaginable and sacred and profane, his city smoke and dust his principalities, his flesh and bone and blood through these cycles and these circuits of heaven even as his limbs and lusts are torn and burned away, so therefore the veil of the temple has been rent asunder and his loosened spirit climbs the sky, trembling electrified and transformative, pulled forcibly loose legs and feet first and dragged up into the heaven, even so therefore his tormentors do see him and they [/call security, get someone up here to take him away]/ and they removed from him his tresses and his skin and his sable enclosure and tonsure at the top of his head which connects him still apparently to this world, and his song is a call that reaches to himself and the vibration of a chord that has been struck which is the string of a magnifical harp the size of infinity and no wider then a zero point, and he sees now that there is no end to the number of ticking trembling points of light that can inhabit any particle of space because there is no space there is only light God's ways are ingenious and as it alway has been is and forever shall be therefore nothing more than his own imperious and self-provoking thought and now here they are the men [who grasp him by the shoulders] they drag him knees scraping drag and pull him up the men who say /what is he doing is he singing/ some men who are come to take him away in dishonor and disgrace, but this is not the first time he has awakened and perhaps it is not the last, for he has seen now not only what and who and when and how, he has seen that it is for the sacred and profane, the darkness and the light, the madness and the sanity and reason, he has seen this time the WHY, which is a single unity of being which diverged into a myriad of forms, a thousand thousands and ten thousand times ten thousand forms, to delight in the very consciousness of being and to awaken and discover itself ten thousand times ten thousand times and as they drag him away in dishonor and disgrace he sees that it is finished now, he sees everything. He knows.

Antiphony

About the author

Chris Katsaropoulos is the author of more than a dozen titles, including two novels, *Fragile* and *Antiphony*. He has traveled extensively in Europe and North America and enjoys collecting music and books. Visit http://antiphonyck.blogspot.com to read more, including a collection of his recent poems.